Early accolades...

"Mark Ruffin's *Bebop Fairy Tales* captures the heart and soul of the American experience during the 20th century with humor, wit and accuracy, just like the solos of the jazz musicians he uses as his artistic muse. It's the best kind of history: poetic, noetic and hip."

—Ben Sidran
Musician, Broadcaster, Author, *The Ballad of Tommy LiPuma*

"In Mark Ruffin's hands, jazz is neither a thing of mystery, nor a distant, misty memory. The music is alive and so are characters who breathe and speak and act out fully realized narratives built on the foundation of jazz legend. These tales may be drawn from the annals of jazz, but they offer enduring lessons of life in America for all of us."

—Ashley Kahn
Author, *Kind of Blue: The Making of the Miles Davis Masterpiece*, *A Love Supreme: The Story of John Coltrane's Signature Album*, and other titles

"With *Bebop Fairy Tales* Mark Ruffin is uniting real people in imagined circumstances that fascinate and captivate the reader. You'll find yourself daydreaming of endless possibilities based on the worlds he's created, you'll be craving for more. He's written a true literary gem."

—Dee Dee Bridgewater
Singer, NEA Jazz Master, 2-time Grammy winner, Memphis Music Hall of Famer

"*Bebop Fairy Tales* is a lively volume, full of engrossing tales and true-to-life stories immersed in the jazz ethic, dressed in the peculiar garments of racial nuances in America and reflections on that most uniquely American pastime baseball, all pointing to the unique impact of jazz on this country's landscape."

—Willard Jenkins
Journalist, Broadcaster, Festival & Concert Producer, Co-Author of *African Rhythms*, the autobiography of NEA Jazz Master Randy Weston

"There have been so many great works of fiction about baseball—*Bang the Drum Slowly*, *The Natural*, and *The Great American Novel* come to mind immediately—but precious few about jazz. Mark shows the impact of race on those institutions and on our culture in 20th-century America. Baseball, jazz and race. Yes, it's a book about America."

—Lee Mergner
Jazz Times

"The world needs Mark Ruffin's *Bebop Fairy Tales* now more than ever. Baseball, Bebop, the drama of life, all together here. Yes, Bebop is the music of the future and these fairy tales teach us the truth."
—Maxine Gordon
Author, *Sophisticated Giant: The Life and Legacy of Dexter Gordon*

"That he can entertain us with these creations, even as they address harsh reality, is a trick as complicated as the chord sequence John Coltrane introduced on *Giant Steps*. And the ability to strike that balance, to run those changes and dole out the dozens—to stitch the things he loves into the thing that threatens—makes *Bebop Fairy Tales* a vibrant tapestry about to unfold."
—Neil Tesser (from his *Introduction*)
Grammy Award-Winning Journalist, Broadcaster, Author

"The author compels us to look at white privilege from multiple angles, and to look at the traumatic malignancy of Black hatred. As well, he nudges us to investigate more closely our own biases—explicit, implicit, or internalized— whether it is toward those of another racial identity or the gay and transgender community, all while telling us some impressive facts about legendary jazzers, sportsmen, and the cities they incarnate. Pretty cool."
—Terri Lyne Carrington (from her *Foreword*)
Founder/Artistic Director, Berklee Institute of Jazz and Gender Justice

BEBOP Fairy Tales

An Historical Fiction Trilogy on Jazz, Intolerance, and Baseball

by Mark Ruffin

Edited by Pat Lofthouse
Art by B'Rael Ali

ISBN 9798663495745

Printed in U.S.A.

Rough In Creative Works
P.O. Box 2821
New York, NY 10027

www.MarkRuffin.com
www.bebop.markruffin.com

Art by B'Rael Ali
www.braelali.com

TABLE OF CONTENTS

Foreword

Remember the pure feeling of gratification you experience when the desired, yet improbable, home run in the 9th inning wins your favorite baseball team's playoff game. Or revisit the thrilling sensation attained when listening to creative improvisers melt together into rhythmic jubilation, creating a sound distinctively identified as jazz. If you have fond recollections of either—or both—then you will find sheer satisfaction in these pages. And if you know American history—even minimally—then you are cognizant of the role intolerance has played in shaping the ongoing justice struggles that help to outline the moral character of the country. How are they related? With fascination and comprehension, Mark Ruffin voices contempt for racial oppression and discrimination based on gender identity, and/or sexual orientation, through the traditions and lifestyles of two important pillars of American culture.

If you've ever met Mark Ruffin, then you would know how fervently he craves and retains information. His attraction to history and rare known facts about jazz is astonishing, but even more fascinating is his in-depth and informative accounts of baseball. Some may ask, "Is this the same Mark Ruffin that I hear on the radio?" given his longtime career as a popular host and program director. But soon, when newcomers run across him at a music event or on the air, they will ask, "Is this the same Mark Ruffin that writes books?" If he had pursued a career in baseball, I believe he would have been a first-rate pitcher, akin to Fergie Jenkins, or Vida Blue, or perhaps Dave Stewart—winning the game by great skill and outsmarting his opponent. As a jazz musician, he would be a star trumpeter; someone with expertise in getting everyone's attention, telling and selling the story, and crafting a poignant point of view on the theme—the same traits that make him a superb author. In any field, Mark Ruffin would be an all-star—no exception here. With this enthralling trilogy, he guides us through the characters' evocative escapades like a skillful snake charmer—his pungi being his pen and his imagination.

I've often used cliché baseball metaphors when teaching the process of learning jazz. I've spoken to students about *heavy hitters* that are *in a league of their own*. I've told them how they have to cover *all the bases* and not *drop the ball*. And what's more, there are the occasional impassioned reprimands about keeping the form of a song: "You came in *out of left field*. You weren't even *in the ball park!*" My novice exploration of baseball site of the church because he knew that by the time they reached the final destination, the music would be even louder.

He didn't know if his head ached from a hangover or from the aggravating fact that he had no money to get to Jackson, let alone back home to Chicago. He was glad he met Viola but she said she had no money to lend him. He suspected that she didn't trust him although she did let him stay in her spacious apartment. Jug had hoped to be long gone by four, the time her white, jealous, police officer boyfriend comes over.

Jug wanted to go home and was pretty tired of Mr. B and his mean ways. He was thinking that exact thought last night on stage at the club in the French Quarter when he spotted Viola in the front row. Their eyes caught at the end of the second chorus of Eckstine singing the song, *I Waited for You*, just before Jug was to stand up from the sax section to take a solo. He pointed at her and mouthed the words "for you" just as he stood up and blew a wail of a chorus.

Ironically, it was Viola at the stage door waiting for a glimpse of Mr. B. Jug was always perceptive with people and he could read his current boss like one of those beginner's music charts Dr. Dyett used to give him back in DuSable High. Jug knew she'd be waiting a long time, but he'd figured the best way to get her attention away from Mr. B was to actually take her in and to have the singer star-fuck her and ignore her like he did any woman with a darker complexion than his.

Viola saw his horn case and remembered him. Jug introduced himself and set it up perfectly, making sure to emphasize how much of an asshole Mr. B really was as he took her backstage. Sure enough, the singer ignored the pretty Viola, especially since she was with Jug. Fortunately, she was resilient and ready to party. They'd hit it off very well over a number of drinks even after she told him of her numerous boyfriends. Jug didn't care, especially when she agreed to take him home. The sex, booze, and pot were all wonderful, but now his head pounded, thinking of a way out of this predicament.

If he didn't get on his way soon, he knew that his sights might have to focus on getting to the Sunday night gig in Memphis.

But I want to see the look of that smug motherfucker's face when I walk in there tonight, Jug thought as he rose to the window, just in time to see the last of the long funeral processional.

Picking up the rear were a number of young boys trying to collect money for the musicians. Jug remembered all the blues musicians who made a living panhandling at the Maxwell Street Market back home. The thought of becoming a semi-permanent member of the crowded music scene in the Crescent City spurred him to say goodbye to Viola and on to finding a way to Jackson.

Two hours later, Jug was lost in New Orleans' West End. The lady who owned the musicians' rooming house told him that Mr. B did take his luggage, for which he was thankful. Walking under the hot Louisiana sun made Jug question his insistence of never leaving his horn anywhere. He loved it while playing in Viola's bedroom but hated it right now. It also came in handy an hour earlier when a woman stopped her car and asked if he needed help. Turned out she liked musicians and gave Jug a ride across town closer to the road on the way to Jackson.

The prospect of hitchhiking through the South was a crazy idea, and he still didn't know if he was serious when his always-smooth-talking tongue backed him into a corner talking to the pretty girl as she drove. She took him as close to West End Boulevard as she was going, let him off, and pointed the way.

"You'll come to a huge park," Jug muttered to himself an hour later, mocking the girl as he walked, his sax case weighing heavier with every step.

"Fuck."

Just then he saw the park straight ahead, and he got a bit homesick.

It was a big beautiful park that rolled gently down a hill that led to Lake Pontchartrain. A half-mile away, he could see the long bridge across the water. It was the road to Jackson, but all he could think about was Grant Park and Lake Michigan in Chicago.

He walked along thinking about the time his father told him how he met Buddy Bolden, the man Albert Ammons said invented jazz.

"Pops said he could blow and be heard clear across Lake Pontchartrain ," he said as he stopped, looking at the massive structure. "Too bad the old boy didn't make any records."

He hummed a line.

"Yeah, the *Blues for Buddy Bolden*."

He fought the urge to pull out his saxophone and instead headed off for Jackson, not knowing that the Big Easy had other plans for him.

Buzz was six years older than Bob and had actually served during the war. He was as ruggedly handsome as Bob was youthful and attractive. Bob had learned enough about the ends and means of gambling through Buzz, that he was sure he could write a book on the subject. Particularly Blackjack. In the ten months since they'd met, Bob, from the very beginning, often wondered why Buzz re-enlisted instead of making a living as a gambler.

Like true friends, the two men had become competitive, even when it came to attracting women. Besides dancing, it was the only area where Bob fared better than his worldly friend.

This time seemed to be different.

Her name was Linda LaLarrimeaux and she was the best-looking woman Bob had seen in five months. Both sailors had spotted her coming down the boulevard, accompanied by a rather plain and frumpy woman. Bob was convinced that even if it were Jane Russell or Betty Grable, all eyes would have still centered on Miss LaLarrimeaux.

She wore a skin-tight, pastel blue with white polka-dots, two-piece suit that she was poured into. The long, wavy black hair was where the curves began, and they didn't stop until the tip of her shoe. As she approached, the two immediately, almost simultaneously, enforced the double-date rule—no matter who got the pretty one, the other had to entertain the less desirable female.

"Double-date," they shouted a beat apart, and laughed.

Bob thought he had nothing to lose. Two hours later, he's in the back seat of Linda LaLarrimeaux' brand-new Cadillac between a basket of wine and cheese, trying to make conversation with her appropriately named sidekick, Jane. Buzz is up front trying to figure out how he's ever going to get Linda out of that dress, and if there was a way he could slide his hand up her legs while she drives.

If he scores, I'll never hear the end of it, echoed through Bob's mind, just as Linda turned into West End Park.

"I know just the place in this here park where both us girls can just let our hair down and have a good ole time with you boys," she said, in that seductively deep Southern tone that had Buzz on the edge of her lips and Bob raging with envy.

"Oh, do you now?" Bob asked, not being able to help the sarcasm as he looked at the scar on the calf on Jane's right leg, just under the hem of her horrid blue and black checkered dress.

"Is there a place just for you and me, sugar?" Buzz purred, turning his head just to get a glimpse of Bob.

"Yes, there's a big stone by a little bush that I just love the smell of," Linda teased, slowing the big machine down as it began a slow cruise through West End Park.

"Hey, Buzz, old pal," Bob said, deliberately cutting her off, "remember that time in the Philippines when you took the heat from Chief Papp for me? We're even."

"Excuse my compadre back there, Linda. He's just a bit jealous..."

"Listen to the way these fellas talk, Linda," Jane blurted, out of her shyness. "They're strange."

"Be nice, Janey girl," Linda replied, before looking at Bob in the rearview mirror. "You should give my friend a chance, Mister. She can show you more than I ever could."

"Oh, I doubt that," Bob said.

"Amen, brother," Buzz said, staring at her medium-sized breasts.

Bob turned and his eyes took a stab at the not very attractive woman he had to entertain as part of the vow with his friend.

"And remember, Cuba."

"Ooh, that was ugly," Buzz replied, scrunching his face and turning to the back for Bob to see. "You can never get even for that."

"Here we are, guys," Linda jumped in, seemingly not interested in losing Buzz's attention for even a few seconds. "Why don't you be a gent and fetch the blankets out of the trunk, Buzzy. I bet all the girls call you Buzzy."

"Yeah, all the girls," Bob gurgled, from the back of the luxury car.

Linda parked the car behind the only other car parked in the vicinity. The street sat on the plateau of a rolling hill. As Bob and Buzz exited the passenger side, they looked up a hill of exquisitely manicured, dark green grass dotted with giant oaks and very tall willows mixed with a number of giant boulders.

The ladies saw the hill continue on across the street, emptying into Lake Pontchartrain. Turning, they saw Buzz dutifully heading for the trunk while Bob was already walking up the hill towards the shade of a rather large oak tree.

"Excuse me, Bob," Linda cried. "Can't you be a gentleman and get the wine and cheese basket, please?"

Bob sheepishly turned to see Buzz's hands filled with blankets.

"I just wanted to help Buzzy find a nice spot," he answered, moving back quickly towards the car.

"That is a terrific spot there," Buzz agreed.

"Yes, let's mosey on over there. But we'll explore over there, Buzzy dear," Linda said, pointing a bit further up the hill towards a huge boulder surrounded by a tall hedge on each side.

"I see, up by that big rock," Buzz responded.

An hour later, Buzz was still trying to get Linda up to that rock.

With what seemed like an unlimited supply of wine, cheese, and crackers, the very prepared Linda LaLarrimeaux plied her guest with the goodies and teased Buzz with the possibilities. The alcohol not only brought Jane out of her shell, but it was her positively witty conversation that kept Linda and Bob enthralled as she rattled on about various topics. She was only slowed by Buzz who looked for reasons to turn his date's attention to the rock up the hill.

Unbeknownst to the quartet, behind the trunk of the giant oak to their right lay sleeping a tired, hungry, and nearly broke black jazz musician. Once, when Buzz mentioned the rock, a subconscious stone came flying towards Jug in his dreams.

He had arrived at this spot from over the hill, right before the picnic unfolded, vowing to take just a short nap. He had been so happy to finally see the lake he had been told to look for that Jug decided to rest before finding the very long bridge yet another stranger told him about. By the time the quartet of cheese and wine revelers arrived, Jug was well past the short nap stage.

Before opening his eyes, Jug fully expected to see a bird overhead about to literally lay waste to him. Once opened, he took the drifting leaves as a sign of his changing luck. He focused in on the lively conversation going on ten yards behind him. His ears honed in just as Buzz's luck was starting to change. Jug heard him mention the rock, and realized he'd been hearing them talking in his dreams for a while.

Jug stood up, dusted off his clothes, opened his saxophone case, and pulled out his suit jacket to put on. As Linda and Buzz headed one way away from Jane and Bob, Jug emerged from behind trees from the other way, headed right towards whatever was left of the wine and cheese.

"I was just thinking, what New Orleans gathering is complete without some music?" a slightly inebriated Jane asked, standing after noticing the black man with the music case coming towards them.

At that moment, Bob thought it quite ironic that the same scene in a Chicago park, in the supposedly more liberated North, would probably cause some amount of fear with a girl back home.

"If he can play some jive, maybe I'll show you a step or two," she continued.

"You show me something, hah!" Bob jumped up and exclaimed. "Ever since that wine has brought you out of whatever hole you were in, you've become quite the confident little lady."

"And a hole is where I'll dance you into."

Her bold demeanor awakened Bob's competitive nature and he actually felt his blood rise.

"Well, I hope you're beyond the Lindy Hop, my little Southern belle, because where I come from we're into modern dance."

"Darling, you're so tall and lanky, you probably trip over

yourself," she countered, sensing that she'd hit a nerve. "Are you sure the wine doesn't have your oars a bit too far in the water, Lieutenant Navy, or Captain Seaman, whatever you are."

Jug barely had a chance to get hello out of his mouth before Bob pounced on him.

"I sure hope you know how to play that thing, because I got a thing or two to show this...."

"Bob, Bob, where are your manners?" Jane asked with a charming smile aimed at Jug. "This is obviously a man of a fine cultured talent who has entered our realm. The least we can do is offer him refreshment."

"Thank you, ma'am," Jug said, grateful that he didn't have to ask.

"Let's just have a seat," she said with a slight laugh while gesturing Jug down to the blanket. "Don't mind him, he needs to stretch his legs."

"And that is supposed to mean what?" Bob asked indignantly.

"What are you doing so far out of the city," Jane asked Jug, ignoring Bob. "Oh, I know, you're one of those musicians who come to practice alone in the park."

"No, it's nothing like that," Jug said sheepishly as Jane opened the basket to the still-plentiful stock of cheese and crackers. "In fact, I need to get to Jackson tonight and I'm looking for some bridge that would put me on the right road."

"What? Are you going to walk?" Jane inquired.

"I thought I could hitchhike."

Jane busted out with a laugh.

"You're going to do what?" she managed between the guffaws.

"You have to excuse her," Bob said, as he sat down and grabbed more wine out of the basket. "This is some really good stuff, and she's a little giddy."

"You're not from around here, are you? No, of course you're not," she went on without a breath.

"Otherwise you would know that New Orleans is a cradle of Southern civility. But the minute a good-looking Negra like you cross that crystal blue lake, your chances of living drops fifty percent."

"You're telling me it's not a good idea, huh."

"So, you're not from around here?" Bob chimed in.

"No, he's not, genius," Jane said, as if annoyed. "Listen to the way he talks."

"No, I'm not from around here," Jug said hopefully as he saw Linda's shiny new car and looked at Bob. "But I'll do anything to get to Jackson tonight. Even pay," Jug answered with a large piece of cheese hanging from his lips.

"Yep, he's a sweet-talking Yankee, just like you, Bobby sock," Jane teased and hiccuped.

"The lady's right. I'm from Chicago. I was..."

"Small world, friend," Bob interrupted, "I'm from the North Side—Irving Park and Ashland."

"Oh, now I bet you think he can really play now, because he's from Chicago," Jane retorted.

"Damn right," came the surprise response out of both Jug and Bob, which shocked the trio into a momentary pause before they erupted in a tension-breaking laughter.

Bob and Jug immediately began searching for some common ground between their lives on completely opposite sides of the second biggest city in the country. As it turned out, Jug had traveled uptown to the North Side to the Aragon Ballroom, and had actually played behind a torch singer at the Green Mill. When Bob told him that he not only knew all about Albert Ammons, but actually owned a player piano roll by Jug's father, he almost spit out the cracker in his mouth.

"That old boogie-woogie piano will never die," Bob said.

"Wish you had one out here, so you could play us a bit," Jane wished.

Jug clapped his hands to clean the crumbs off of them and began to open up his saxophone case.

"Well, a piano would have killed me carrying it around in this hot sun," Jug said smugly. "Besides, I got this saxophone."

"Okay, well let's swing then," Jane exclaimed, standing up as Jug did.

Bob just glared up at her, not taking her bait. He had to be convinced that this was more than just the son of an aging boogie-woogie star. He needed music to move him to dance. He had noticed this personal idiosyncrasy years ago when he was a young kid.

He had hated Benny Goodman's hit, *Sing, Sing, Sing*. When he tried to dance to music that he didn't like, he felt uncomfortable, like he was outside his body watching himself look foolish. He remembered that Dorothy Johnson, whom he had a devastating crush on, loved Goodman. The song was nearly eight minutes long.

Bob was smiling, in a daze looking up at Jug and Jane, but his mind was on those early junior high days, when even eight minutes on a dance floor alone with Dorothy Johnson wasn't enough to get him to dance to music he didn't like.

The smile broadened.

While trying to find a tempo and think of what to play, Jug was unconsciously rocking back and forth with his horn in his mouth. Not a sound was emerging, but Jane rocked unconsciously in his rhythm.

"Come on, get on with it," Jane excitedly shouted, looking down at Bob, bringing him back to the present.

When Jug did start playing, the music literally jolted Bob straight up off his feet. The saxophonist had unleashed a torrent of notes as a three-quarter bar pickup to a romping, barreling, boogie-woogie tune. In the instant that he lit into the first full bar of the song, Bob was staring at him. His face still but his body steeped in the hot rhythm Jug was laying down.

Bob marveled at what was essentially only a short staccato bass line Jug was doing. Jug stomped his foot in the frenetic four-four time as he played, while Bob, still staring, had his legs going every which way in perfect double-time. After eight bars, Jug shifted into the opening lines of the melody and then he went back to the bass line between the phrases, seemingly without taking a breath. A shout emanated from Bob's gut. The sound worked its way to his throat, and a loud "woo" blurted out his mouth and nose. He did a perfect 360 and jerked his head back away from Jug.

That's when he noticed Jane.

She had moved away from the wine and was bent down, moving her arms up and down and her neck back and forth like a chicken. He realized she was doing a version of a dance he had seen old Lindy Hoppers do. But it was different.

As he was trying to remember the dance, she hunched over towards him with her limbs flailing and perfectly in sync with Jug. Suddenly she stood up straight, clapped her hand, did her own 360, and right as Jug was finishing the downbeat of a measure, Jane shouted, "Let's dance."

Bob grabbed her hand in time, and they were off.

Jug felt as if he was watching a movie, but he was in it and the three of them were generating a lot of energy.

From behind the rock, the sound of the saxophone came just in the nick of time for Linda, as Buzz's heavy petting was getting a bit too heavy. She jumped up and looked around the rock. Buzz was incredulous when he followed seconds later and saw Bob dancing.

"That fucker Fosse," he muttered, then mocked him, "the last thing I want to do is dance."

Neither Buzz, Linda, nor the trio of performers noticed the limousine that had parked two cars ahead of Linda's. The huge Packard

She winked at him. "Ain't that right, Buzz?"

Buzz knew that he had just seen a ghost.

The moist, warm night air of New Orleans was as intoxicating to Jug as the drinks he had consumed at the Linton mansion. He began to feel really comfortable with the obvious advances Delilah was making towards him. The two of them were so absorbed in the sexual tension and double entendre games they were playing, they hardly noticed how quiet the other two passengers were.

Bob was also getting high off the sights, sounds, and smell of the Crescent City as the hearse segued from the Garden District, through downtown, toward the French Quarter, Poydras and St. Charles. The city had him so entranced that Bob wasn't paying attention to the two in front or his silent partner.

There was music everywhere: in nightclubs, on the street, in hotel parlor windows, from radios blasting through the French architecture.

Buzz was comatose. The chill never went away and he didn't utter a word.

Through the ride his nerves were on edge as he thought about the eyeball and the hearse he was riding in. He could hear the liquid in the back of the hearse swishing as loud as the ocean in his cousin's beach house back in Malibu.

"Poison," he almost whispered aloud.

He didn't hear the piano trio passing the hotel or the loud blues of Ida Mae Cox belting through the French Quarter. The Dixieland band in the street that Bob so enjoyed and Delilah almost hit was like a blur to Buzz, as he couldn't shake the feeling that the woman driving was a witch and that she was on a mission tonight.

When Delilah made a wide right onto Rampart Street, Buzz leaned into the window and was startled by a street merchant on the corner selling voodoo dolls.

He looked down toward his feet and saw Jug's saxophone case between him and Bob.

Suddenly, he was himself.

A chuckle came out of his mouth as he felt the thick wad of money in his pocket. Buzz stared at the case and desperately wanted nothing more than to play his trombone.

The turn down the decidedly residential street also brought Bob out of his tourist-like haze.

"Where ya' been buddy," Bob asked of his fellow member of the

Navy. "You were like out."

"Whaddya' mean, out?" Buzz tartly responded.

"Ole Buzzy was just in a trance, Bob," Delilah butted in, looking at Bob in the rearview mirror.

"That's right," Buzz said rather agreeably to Delilah, not showing any ill will. "Just taking in all New Orleans has to offer."

"Just don't get in any trouble tonight, you two. And if possible, stay within eyesight of me, especially you, Jug," she said, turning to him in front, adding, "and bring your horn."

"What kind of trouble?" Jug asked. "It's just a party, and the way you describe it, it sounds like one of those South Side rent parties we always have in Chicago."

"Just be careful. That's all I'm asking."

Bob and Buzz looked at each other and shrugged their shoulders.

"And Buzzy," Delilah continued. "You will get to play, like never before."

The place was just rattling with music, even before the quartet reached the stoop and short flight that led into an old three-flat. Horns, in unison, blared out a boogie-woogie line that had a stop-start syncopation to it that led to the dancers in the crowd screaming "Yeah!" every fourth measure.

With one hand holding his sax case, Jug started snapping his other fingers just as Bob looked up to admire the old French architecture of the building and Buzz's pulse rate went up. Jug bounded up the stairs but waited for Delilah to gain entry. She smiled at him as she took her time, with Jug and Bob bouncing rhythmically in tow.

Her blue eyes began to glow as did the broach around her neck, and Buzz got what was now becoming a familiar chill when he got too close to Delilah. The smile became almost sinister to him, and he stepped back towards the door.

In perfect synchronization, it opened just as Delilah reached it.

A little young miss said, "Come in, please."

"Hello, Dominique, don't we look lovely?" Delilah crooned, slightly chuckling at Buzz.

"Why, thank you, Miss D," she replied. "I'm the belle of the ball."

She was a shapely woman in her early 20s wearing a long soft pink satin dress with a white cotton slash draped around it, bearing the words "Miss Rampart" stenciled in purple. Buzz stared at her as Bob and Jug entered behind their hostess.

Buzz entered a hallway with a flight of stairs on the right and a

Billy Eckstine's band?"

"Yep, that's right," Jug shouted. "I'm not quite ready, but my buddy here can handle a 'bone pretty good. Got an ax for him?

"We'll find one," he said, before turning to the band. "Okay guys, let's jump bluesy in D, rhythm first, boys. Let's go, one, uh two, a three—a one two three four."

In the kitchen, Jug and Bob were greeted by the smell of barbecue and fried fish. Delilah was being hugged by a big, black busty woman in an apron. There were two couples eating at a small table and a white woman behind one of those pantry doors where the bottom is closed and the top open. Heat was emanating from the oven but there were no pots cooking over the eyes of the stove. This was something both Bob and Jug noticed right away.

"Miss D, honey, we all've been waiting for you all night," the black busty one said in an extended Southern drawl.

"Yeah, they don't go for my potions the way they go for yours," the one dressed in black said.

"Porky Pie Jones just brought it up, and that child over there couldn't wait to start stirring it up," she said, walking up to the boys.

"These are special friends of mine," Delilah introduced them. "The dark, extremely handsome one is Jug, and his rail-thin friend is Bob."

"Well, he's rail-thin because he hasn't had enough to eat, honey. I'm Beulah," she said, shaking Bob's hand and then grabbing the saxophone case from Jug. "Here, let me take this thing until you've put something into that stomach."

The same young couple at the door came through the kitchen.

"Excuse us, Miss Beulah, we're starving," the man said, cutting a path through the women on both sides and going straight to the kitchen and out another door.

"I'll take that, Beulah," Delilah said of the case, "You show them the food. You two check in with me from time to time. I'll always be right here."

Then she reached over and gave Jug a wet kiss on his lips.

Beulah led the two out to the porch where three men were sitting on a railing with plates of food. Beyond them, on each side of the yard, were men and women cooking in steel drums. There were ten small serving stations in all, with tables for four or five at each. More men were coming down the stairs to the right which caught Bob's attention again.

"What's upstairs?" Bob's curiosity piqued in.

"Oh, we do a little gaming on the third floor," Beulah replied innocently. "And there's a red-light room on the second floor. That's two dollars more for that party and five dollars to win you a little money on the top floor."

The men filed by Beulah, all with a nod or smile to the matron.

"It's a dollar to eat; you pay Dale down there."

Bob followed the gamblers down to the yard and turned to Jug. "Don't tell Buzz about the little gaming. I'd hate for him to lose that roll."

"Well, he's been on some kind of roll."

Jug had a big salad, shrimp, catfish, jambalaya, kidney stew, green beans, and sweet potatoes. Bob had chicken, shrimp, okra, rice and gumbo, corn on the cob, and peach cobbler. He was halfway through his meal, talking about his day, when Jug got up for seconds of catfish, ribs, etouffee, potato salad, and more sweet potatoes. Bob bought each of them a huge mug of New Orleans beer.

After putting down such a prodigious meal, the stout Chicagoan stood up and patted the big bony shoulders of his new white friend from home. "Now I'm ready to go show these folks from Louisiana how we blow at a house party."

They walked back into the kitchen to see Delilah behind the door where the woman in the black dress was. A line including four men and a woman were left waiting when she reached to give Jug his saxophone.

"What are you selling?" Bob asked.

"I'm just helping Beulah get her rent paid, dispensing my worldly advice on love with the added insurance of my grandmother's magic love elixir. You see somebody you want tonight, Bobby, you come on over, and I'll fix you up right special."

Buzz was having quite the musical experience. At first, horrified that he was being called on to play without sheet music in front of him, he had adapted to the on-the-spot arranging that was being so masterfully done by Mack, the various singers who've gotten up to sing with the band, and the rest of the gentlemen playing horns around him.

On the sixth number, the saxophone player, who had introduced himself as Little Pistol, told him to modulate the line they were playing behind a very fat blues singer. By that time, Buzz could almost feel the musical change coming. The energy coming from the dancers in the mostly black crowd was nothing like what he was accustomed to doing at USO and special shows for troops.

After his seventh number with the group, Mack asked Buzz if he wanted to take a break. "Hell no," was his answer. The last time Buzz dancing with Teas just as he was about to tear into a wicked solo on the Eckstine ballad when the commotion started. He was enjoying being the guest star with the fine group of musicians surrounding him and, though he'd never admit it to anyone, he felt a twinge of jealousy as Jordan approached the stage.

"Hey, Mack," Jug shouted to Mack, who was grooving to the boogie-woogie the rhythm section was playing as a bed while Jordan made his way up front. "I ain't going nowhere."

Jug figured he had his alto horn. Jordan, who didn't play tenor, would have to borrow someone's alto. It wouldn't be his, he reasoned. Besides, Jug was already contemplating the riffs he would instantaneously compose as Jordan began singing.

"I'm gonna cut Louis Jordan tonight," he boasted to Mack. "That is, if he even plays his horn."

Both musicians laughed.

The pace of the men quickly changing positions in the horn section reflected the seasoning that comes with years of participating in impromptu or planned jam sessions in New Orleans. There were four completely different trumpet players. Counting Jug, two of the alto players stayed while three changed hands. The two tenors were replaced with three new ones. The rhythm guys were obviously staying as the pianist, drummer, and bassist all patiently grooved until Jordan and the horns were settled. A new guitarist did plug in his amplifier and three of the four trombone players left, including Buzz.

"What's the white boy's name?" asked Mack as he leaned into Jug.

"Buzz," Jug replied.

"Good swinging there, Buzz," he shouted over the din, before turning to reach for Jordan's hand to whisper in his ear.

"Okay, boys," Mack said, turning to his fresh squad of players. "You know the opening riff; just follow Jug here with a call and response after that until we find something else."

He looked over his shoulder to Jordan who was playing to the crowd with his exaggerated facial antics.

"On the downbeat, fellas," he said, nodding to Jordan. "A one, two, a one two three four..."

"Caldonia," Jordan screamed into the microphone that was plugged into the same source as the guitarist.

The horns thumped.

"Caldonia, what makes your big head so hard?"

The crowd exploded.

Buzz was in the kitchen by the time the other trombonists started. Mack's praise of "Good swinging there!" was still ringing in his ears.

Standing against a wall, Buzz stared out in space, thinking back to the show he did with Rita Hayworth and how Chief Papp chose him to be featured throughout the performance. He had considered it his musical zenith until this night. Marveling at the disparity in the two moments, Buzz laughed and almost knocked the drink out of a woman's hand as he clapped his.

He thought about how scripted to the second the Hayworth routine was, while he could barely keep up with this band where there wasn't even any sheet music. He chuckled again, thinking how he wasn't featured at all here in New Orleans yet he knew this was the best musical night of his life. Being classically trained and then ingrained with big band–era charts in college and the military, Buzz never quite understood the compose-on-the-fly attitude of the jazz musician; that is, until now.

"*I became a jazz musician tonight,*" he thought, just as he felt that familiar chill.

When Buzz woke out of his daydream, he was looking directly into Delilah's mysterious brooch. She was across the kitchen, in the pantry exchanging a dollar bill for a ladle full of the strange liquid she'd transported. There was no sign of the eyeball in the brooch, for which Buzz felt grateful. The blue color seemingly became dotted with clouds and Buzz was transported into some private sky emanating from a tiny brooch twenty feet away from him.

"And Buzzy, you will get to play like never before."

It was Delilah's voice, but playing directly into his head. He never saw Beulah approach him.

"Come on, honey, Miss D says I've got to take good care of you," the old lady said. "She said you had a apifany or something like that. Sounds like something that'll make you hungry, so let me show you the food, honey."

Out of his hypnotic state, he tilted his head up to see the huge smile of Delilah directed right at him.

"You know, Miss, I'm not really hungry," Buzz said, sending an instant show of disappointment on Beulah's face. "But I can go for some of that chocolate cake I've seen folks come out of here with."

"Just follow me, sir."

Buzz never saw that chocolate delight, for as soon as he and Beulah stepped out to the back porch, Buzz was distracted by a man coming down the stairs counting money.

"I see you're enjoying yourself, Mr. St. John," Beulah said to the

"I'm sort of her guest here," Bob said, now leading Teas.

But she let go of his hand. Jug had noticed it before, how some people seemed to prepare themselves before approaching Delilah. Now he watched Teas brush her dress, fuss her hair, and generally get ready to be received by the mysterious white lady.

"Well Bob, I see you're enjoying yourself," she said, as Jug thought that it wasn't the general on-edge sheepish-like submission some Southern blacks employ when they're around a powerful white person.

"Come try some of Dee's love juice," Jug said, deciding that it was more like they're on guard to try to curry her favor.

"Now who is this pretty N'awlins queen you have latched onto, Bob?"

"I'm Teas, the daughter of Lucy Grimes," she replied, before Bob could say a word.

"She used to work for you back right before the war in the 30s," she said, as Jug snickered when Teas did a slight genuflect.

"Oh yeah, good ol' Lucy, fast learner. Your mama ain't been up to see me in a few months. You tell her to come up and see me."

Teas saw the brooch around Delilah's neck turn sky blue. Then an eye winked. She smiled, certain only she saw the vision.

"Teas, you treat my friend Bob here well," she said, rising to go back to the pantry where an older black woman was dispensing the potion to all comers.

"Shit Dee, you should have seen these two on the dance floor," Jug said from the table. "Bob had this girl on a boogie-woogie merry-go-round."

"Bob tells me all you guys from Chicago dance like that," Teas said to Jug.

"Honey, Bob meant all white guys," Jug said with a hearty laugh, patting his horn case. "The only dancing I'm doing is with this horn."

"Speaking of Chicago, if we're going to get our friend here on his way to Memphis, we're going to be leaving soon," Delilah said, rejoining the group and thrusting a cup into Bob's hands.

"What's this," Bob asked.

"Just drink it," Jug insisted.

"What is it?"

"Just drink it."

"It's a...call it a facilitator," Delilah said, sitting down. "That's another good word."

"Facilitator, hah?" Jug snorted. "It's Love Juice, a sex potion, a dick hardener."

Bob looked down into the blue liquid and began blushing. He shrank at the thought that Jug and Delilah knew he had sex on his mind with Teas.

"What make you think I need something like that?"

The reflexes of Teas kicked in before she knew she had nudged Bob. Delilah and Jug laughed, and she blushed right along with Bob.

"That settles it. Drink up, Bobby boy," Jug said, giggling.

"What's in it?"

"Don't worry about it, Bobby," Jug laughed harder. "It's government-approved. Hell, they'll be selling it in stores in the future. I can see it now, Dee's Syrup, in the little blue bottle, at Rexall Drug Stores everywhere."

"Bob, you and Buzz are big boys," Delilah said, stifling her laughter. "'What say we leave you two on your own so I can get started on up to Memphis. Your hotel ain't too far away from here and Teas can get you to a cab."

"For all I know, Buzz is already back at the hotel," Bob said, finally downing the liquid in one gulp.

"Naw, Buzz is alright," Delilah informed Bob. "He's up on the third floor. Like I said, I'm sure Teas will get both of you back together."

"Thank you, Delilah," Bob countered, reaching down to kiss her on the cheek. "We've had a great time."

"When you get back home, look me up," Jug said from across the table. "I'm always at some club on the South Side when I'm home."

"I'm gonna do that."

"And tell that crazy partner of yours to always watch out for those girls with three legs."

Bob paused and looked at Jug quizzically for a beat. Then he laughed.

Teas said goodbye and pulled Bob along out of the kitchen and up the back stairs porch.

"So your mom used to work for Delilah," he said, suddenly feeling flushed even though it was much cooler outside.

"Yeah, it was more like school and running errands for your pay."

"How zat?" Bob slurred.

"Well, you know Miss Dee is a witch, don't ya?" Teas asked, looking down at Bob from the middle landing.

"Not a real witch, mind ya. Not like those voodoo doctors on the levee and in the swamps. She just knows everything about dose 'erbs and potions. My mother's a healer. She can't mess with spirits like Miss Dee."

"Uh-huh," Bob said, feeling glad that Teas was feeling talkative because he was feeling feverish.

"You sound like a nonbeliever," Teas opined in a sassy tone. "That's okay, some people don't believe. Some do even if they say they don't."

She swung open the screen on the back of the second-floor door. The swirl of air from the door hit Bob like a gigantic palm fanning one gigantic wave. The beads of sweat on his forehead felt like tiny icicles and, suddenly, Teas's breasts were the most delectable items he had ever seen.

"Sorry, gal. There's no mo' room up heah. Go down and have yo' sef 'nother drank, come back later," said a strong willful voice that shook Bob out of his trance.

He looked up and saw what he instantly thought was one of the ugliest women he had ever laid eyes on. And she was purple. Bob jerked his head back and staggered, more taken aback than intoxicated.

"But Cathy, this here man is a friend of Miss Dee's," Bob heard Teas say as he looked into the apartment where every lightbulb was painted a strange kind of dark blue. He realized that it was a light above the woman Teas called Cathy that gave her very dark skin the purple hue.

"I don't care who this white man be," the woman replied as she stood up off the stool where she sat guarding the door. "We ain't got no room, we got no room."

"Okay, then, how 'bout we pay double, you find us something then?" Teas asked, turning to Bob. "How much money you got, honey?"

Bob immediately theorized that maybe he had more money in his pocket than he'd probably had at one time ever in his life.

"Oh, a little," he responded, reaching into his pocket and gingerly picking out just a few bills from his folded-up wad.

It was three twenty-dollar bills. Teas's eyes lit up and she snatched them from Bob's hand. "I'll take those."

She handed one to Cathy.

"Oh, we'll make somebody move," she said, opening the door and showing them in. Then she stopped, as if changing her mind. "Naw, I can't do that. But I got the place for you. It's small, but private."

As Bob entered the dark glow, he heard a woman moan from behind the closed door of the room that would've been the pantry downstairs. He could've sworn he saw Teas's butt relax when he heard the same female sigh again.

He looked up and saw a menacing figure coming from the

other side of the even darker hallway. As it got closer, Bob pulled Teas to him and put his head into her neck from behind, watching the guy walk towards him. He couldn't believe his first hunch, but it was Caleb Stinson, the racist Kentuckian from the boat. With his nose down, hoping not to be recognized, Bob watched him walk by. Teas stroked his face.

"Can't we have the space he had?" Teas asked.

"Now, guhl, you seen dat man done come up heah by hisself. He was up in da red-light room."

"What does that mean?" Bob asked, still deep in Teas's neck.

"That means he likes boys," Cathy huffed, coming up short of the door where she obviously was leading them to. "Now you don't know that white man, so you'se let him do what he wan' and mind yo' own beeswax."

She opened the door to a spacious room with more painted blue lights.

"What the hell is this, Cathy? My time ain't up," said the man in bed, hovering over a woman who was in a compromising position but still reached for sheets to cover up.

"I know that, Junior Boyd," Cathy shouted back to the man. "Dese heah white man is a friend of Miss Dee, and dis girl heah is Lucy Grimes dau'ter, and I's knows you don' wanna trouble from dem, do ya?

"I'ma jus' put dem heah in dis closet, ya won' even knows dey dere."

Bob looked at the woman in dismay as she said closet, but he sure wasn't about to challenge her considering she was ordering Junior Boyd, more than suggesting or asking.

She opened a door to a long narrow closet filled with clothes. She pulled back dresses in both directions.

"Now, dat's all I got. You do da bizness dere and get off my nerves."

Teas rolled her eyes at the woman and looked at Bob. After a beat, she looked back into the closet where it recessed into a well beyond the hinges of the nearest door.

"No, I have a better idea," she said.

She pulled the dresses the other way, making a space against the back wall. She left a few dresses obviously making a cushion to stand against.

"Now Bob, you go stand there, and Cathy, you push those dresses back and close the door and go on."

Teas entered sensually towards Bob in the ensuing darkness. Cathy did what she was told as they heard her talking and laughing as she left the room.

the raid started.

As the pair hit the stairs from the stoop, a gunshot rang out from the third floor.

"Oh, shit," Delilah exclaimed, "I've lost Buzz."

The only reason Buzz entered the United States Navy was because his father, a big-time Hollywood musician contractor, demanded it and greased the skids. He knew his hitch was with the musician branch of Special Forces. It was the place that was going to, according to his father, "make him a musician who could earn a living." This Saturday night fish fry was the first battle Buzz had seen. And he was scared.

The fighting on the third floor was much more intense. The biggest and brawniest of the cops came up to rumble the toughest and roughest of the gamblers, cheaters, and killers on this side of New Orleans. Knives clashed with clubs and fists. The thud of bodies being punctured and pelted blended in with the terrific shouts of near joy at afflicting pain and the horrific screams of those on the receiving end.

Buzz noticed the eye even before the first cop had reached the third level.

Near the ceiling of the room surrounded by a haze that was the exact same color as the brooch around Delilah's neck, Buzz felt an immediate familiarity with the floating white iris. The pupil was of a darker blue that seemed to beckon Buzz and gave him the immediate notion that had he reacted when he first saw it, he would've had a better chance of escaping the impending chaos.

Buzz still wasn't startled at all by the sudden vision above his head. Instead, he saw it as a sign of luck, considering the roll he was on.

The eye winked and so did Buzz.

"Wha' da fuck ya winkin' at, mudderfucker?" the houseman scolded. "Throw the dice."

Buzz threw a ten, the number he needed in the craps game. He was reaching for his pot of money when the ruckus started.

"Shit, it's a raid," the houseman said, leaping for the pot.

The two met lunging for dollars when the fight began. That's when the eye moved off the wall to right above the houseman's head. That sudden move did startle Buzz and he jumped back.

The eye jumped to the far wall and Buzz was transfixed. He instinctively knew he was to follow. He tried to get up, but a man fell over him, pushing him back down to the ground. He turned over to see a policeman reaching down for him. He crawled left, towards the eye, the policeman went right after the guy who fell.

Crawling to the wall, another cop tripped over him. For a split second they were eye to eye, and Buzz saw the rage in the man's eyes. The eye rose on the wall and moved towards the front; so did Buzz. The cop pursuing him was jumped on, just a second away from having enough time to reach for Buzz's collar.

The eye went down under the fracas. Buzz followed, not realizing he'd ducked the nightstick of a cop aimed at his head. In fact, there was an air of calm emanating from Buzz as he casually followed the eye to the front. He wasn't even thinking how he was getting past the monster of an Irish cop guarding the front door.

Trust Delilah, he was thinking when he heard the gunshot from behind him. He turned towards the sound, losing sight of the eye. When he turned back towards the door, he couldn't locate the eye. Now fear engulfed him. He looked up just as a billy club came across his head. Buzz was knocked out. His last action before losing consciousness was feeling the lump of cash in his pocket.

"What do you mean, you lost Buzz?" asked Jug, who was now guiding the pair quickly across the street after the gunshot.

"You wouldn't understand if I told you, Jug," Delilah replied. "You see, New Orleans is a bit different and we do things a bit different down here."

"What the hell does that have to do with losing Buzz?" Jug continued questioning.

They were now safely ensconced across the street watching the mass arrest along with many who got out mixed with the curious neighbors across the street.

"Look," she said, turning her gaze away from the action directly to Jug, "if you guys weren't guests of my father and had I not got those guys into this jam, I'd leave right now, and we'd head off…"

"Slow down, Delilah, I'd rather help them than leave, if we can. But what can we do?" Jug responded over the voice of a self-righteous woman next to them who was espousing the brave duty of the police officers.

"Oh, we can do something, my darling Jug. Like I said, this is New Orleans, something can be done," she responded, with her voice trailing and her gaze now over Jug's shoulder. "What we've got to do is find my brother. He can help."

Jug turned to see what had Delilah's attention, and saw a jeep parked down the street with two military police officers sitting in it.

"Sometimes military brass offers the police special bounties on until my friend gets out of jail."

"But darling, you know I need that account straightened out up there."

"I know, darling baby brother, and I'm onto it, after you do this for me, please."

"Oh, okay, but you need about a thousand dollars, and how does she know what he looks like?" Jamie asked.

"It sounds like they've met already," Delilah said with a laugh.

The ride to the jail wasn't very far from where the bunch was arrested. Buzz was quite surprised to find the lockup was right in the French Quarter. It was right before the guards opened the wagon that he heard a prisoner say the name of the judge he was going to see.

"Jus' a lil' sleep fellas befoe' we sees Sunrise Sammy," said the drunken and bruised gambler sitting across from his hard cold bench in the wagon.

"That would be Judge Sunrise Sammy Garrison," the high-cultured Southerner said at the end of the row. He was not only the sole white man from Dixie, he was the only civilian among the Caucasians.

Buzz had noticed the man people called Ski when he was gambling. Ski was the only white man who gamed with the hard-core gamblers, talking as loud as they did and threatening violence almost as much. But he did it in a proper, intoned style that left the recipient chilled. He was as funny as he was refined and obviously as ruthless as he was skilled. In the patrol wagon, it was Ski who purposely took the heat off of Stinson when the black prisoners were poking him because of the racist views Buzz told them about.

"He'll see all you Navy boys first, of course," Ski said, as the door was being opened. "Because everybody gets paid when you boys go to jail, the coppers, the guards, and the judge."

"What do you mean by that?" asked one Navy prisoner.

"You'se guys has got a bounty on your ass," came a black voice from the other side of the bench.

"That's right, and everybody gets a cut," Ski concurred.

"Okay, get your asses up and out," a brawny cop said at the door. "Don't take your fucking time and don't start any fucking shit or you will get your ass kicked inside."

The band was marched into the back of the building, up a flight of stairs into a small booking area. One guard took off the handcuffs, another took their information and personal items, making them count their money carefully. Buzz had $1,989.37.

Two big cops pointed the way straight into two massive holding cells, while still another cop guided them into their respective cells. They were carefully segregated with black prisoners in one cell and the white in the other.

When Buzz was ushered in right behind Stinson, he looked up to about thirty faces. Before he finished looking around, Ski came up behind him.

"I figured you weren't thinking they were going to do this, huh?"

"What do you mean?" Buzz inquired.

"Separate us. You weren't thinking when you were blabbing on about how your Navy buddies love the Negroes, were you?

"What difference does it make?" Buzz snapped.

"Let's just say on this side of the room I don't think anyone cares what you two got going."

"Soooo?"

"Well, he'll realize that soon and you're going to have some trouble."

Buzz felt very alone when he turned back around to face the front of the room. The black faces across in the other cell felt a lot friendlier than the white one close to him. He took a deep breath and then realized no one in either room was paying any attention to him.

"I've got to get out of here, tell me about this judge, when we gonna see him?"

"Boy," Ski laughed, "you going from one hoosegow to another. Them Navy boys gonna be waiting on your ass at the courtroom door."

"Shit."

"If you gotta do that, it's over there where the queers hang," Ski said, pointing and laughing.

Buzz looked up to see the dirty commode. Four guys were standing around it. Two were obviously homosexuals. Some men were finding room against the wall to sleep. Others milled about and mumbled among each other. Things were much livelier in the black cell. The two big guards in the middle ignored both groups.

"So, you're telling me I'm screwed?"

"Pretty much, son," Ski replied. "Now I don't have a hell of a lot of experience in here, but once I did see the coppers let a guy come in here and just pick a bunch of guys out of here and they let them go.

"He was a white man," Ski continued, "but half the folks he got out were black."

"I've seen that happen before too," said a man standing next to them who neither were aware of, "but the guy I saw come got all those he-shes out."

Bob about the eye that almost guided him out of the raid.

"The girl I was with said Delilah is a witch, and she was serious," Bob informed his buddy.

"Well, I don't know about that, but there is some kind of magic going on," insisted Buzz, before stopping and reflecting for a beat.

"You and Jug seemed to love her," he continued. "The woman gave me the creeps every time she was anywhere near me."

Delilah was on the other side of town savoring coffee discussing Buzz and Bob with Jug, mostly how innocent she thought they were. She told him more about the way things were done in New Orleans, how her brother and his friends have frequent trysts with men in high places, and how blackmail is a frequent form of payment. She told him explicitly decadent and troubling stories about Linda LaLarrimeaux.

Over breakfast the young Linton moved into her family's history with tales of how her father and grandfather made their fortunes during Prohibition. Afterwards, they went into the legitimate distribution business and now deliver alcohol, food, and hotel and restaurant supplies all over the Southeast.

She explained how the eldest Linton taught her and Jamie the business and how, despite his appearance and lifestyle, he's the best vice-president of operations her family's growing company has ever had. Inventory and accounting, thanks to four years at the University of Mississippi business school, was her specialty in the family business.

"Daddy always taught us that money was power and that the Lintons had a lot of both," she purred. "It was my mother dear who taught Jamie and me the power of sex."

"What do you mean by that?" Jug asked through a mouthful of well-scrambled eggs.

"Oh, you know what I mean," she said sassily, "and if you don't you're going to find out before you head home to Chicago."

Delilah finished the breakfast with seductive talk filled with suggestive innuendo and sensual movements. By the time they got back to her hearse, she had Jug utterly mystified with a whole different kind of magic than she used with Buzz. With an impending separation, Jug felt no pressure and decided he was going to take advantage of her teasing offers.

"But, Delilah dear," he queried, right after they started their seven-hour journey to Tennessee's largest city, "we're riding through the heart of Dixie. Just how are you planning on, as you said, giving me the best carnal and material experience possible?"

"Hey, I've got about fifteen hours till you get on that bandstand tonight," she countered. "You don't worry about a thing. Just sit back, let me handle it. Relax and enjoy the ride."

That's just what Jug did. He slept all the way to Memphis. He didn't wake up when she made a restroom stop, a gasoline fill-up stop, or when she stopped right outside of town to amend her hotel reservations. Jug was dreaming he was hitting Billy Eckstine on top of the head when he was wakened by a knock on the window.

"Excuse me, sir," prodded a pimply-face white kid in a bellboy's uniform.

Jug snapped his head up and tried to clear the cobwebs in his head before looking at the driver side to see Delilah wasn't there. Before rolling down the window, he saw a sign behind the boy that said, "Loading Dock, Peabody Hotel."

"Yes," he said in as dignified a manner as possible. "You're Miss Linton's accountant, right? She's going to meet you behind that door over there. She gave me the keys and I'm getting her bags out of the back."

Jug looked at the short landing where the door was next to the dock. He slowly got out of the car as the kid opened the back door and pulled out his saxophone case.

"Oh, I'll get that," Jug said.

"That's okay. Miss Linton told me how you're from up North and how we should try to treat you different. You know, not like a nigger from down 'round here."

"Is that what she said now?" Jug teased.

"Oh no, that's not what she said, not like that, she just..."

"That's okay, *boy*," he said. "I'll still take my own case."

"If you insist," the bellboy said with some intensity in his voice. "She's right up there, you go on and meet her."

Jug walked away with his saxophone case, muttering under his breath.

"Racist ass white trash," he whispered to himself, walking towards the stairs.

"Uppity fucking nigger," the bellboy snickered under his breath at the back of the hearse.

Delilah met a steaming Jug on the other side of the dock door.

"Same old not-in-the-front-door Negra kind of shit, huh massa," Jug vented in a Southern accent. Then he put his case down the long way, put his elbows down, palms up and planted his face in the middle. "I can even be yo' lawn jockey if you like."

"Come on Jug, honey," Delilah sighed exhaustedly, grabbing Jug next few hours. He smiled easily when he realized, from Memphis until their tour bus pulled into St. Louis, band mates were going to be paying tribute to him for his accomplishments; Delilah, the Peabody Hotel, and making Mr. B look stupid.

Out the door and into the sunshine, Jug was strolling and feeling better with each stride. Then his mouth dropped, when he looked up and saw the police car. He stopped for an instant when he saw the bellboy talking to the officer outside the Billy Eckstine tour bus.

"Don't worry," Delilah said to him.

Inside the tour bus, the driver had been worried about the cop on his tail who just sat in the car. When the bellboy came out running and the cop got out of the car, the driver wanted to pull away, but Mr. B told him to wait. Dexter Gordon, Art Blakey, Wardell Gray, Fats Navarro, Oscar Pettiford, Mr. B, and the rest of the band saw Jug walk out of the hotel arm in arm with Delilah, and they began cheering, even though, for many, it meant a loss of some cash.

"Get a load of this fucking shit, would ya," stammered Eckstine.

"That's him, that's him," shouted the bellboy once he saw the managers and his co-workers follow the offending couple out the hotel door.

"Relax son, I'll handle this," the cop told the boy as Jug and Delilah approached them. "Good day, Delilah."

The tension Jug had been experiencing dropped like melted butter in a frying pan with that greeting. He knew the fix was in and in defiance, he turned around towards the approaching Peabody Hotel employees and stuck out his tongue at them. He thought this tasted a little bit like freedom.

"The gentlemen on this bus are the gentlemen in question, right?" the brawny officer asked her, walking them to the front of the bus.

"Officer, officer," the clerk supervisor shouted as he got closer to them. "This Negra here had the audacity to enter our hotel."

"Look, I'll handle this," the cop once again replied coolly. "You folks go on back to work now, you hear."

Before the policeman could knock on the front door of the bus, it opened. Jug got on first, then Delilah and the officer, who ordered the driver to close the front door.

"Now, which one of you boys is the Mr. B that's on the side of this here bus?"

"That's him, right here, Jimmy," Delilah pointed.

"Okay, Mr. B," said the policeman, "you settle the score with this young lady here and you can be on your way."

The band members on the bus exploded, screaming accolades and plaudits to Jug. Mr. B reached in his pocket and pulled out a wad of bills. Delilah took half of what Mr. B gave her and gave it to Jug, which elicited more applause. She gave the other half to the cop she called Jimmy.

"Now, I'm just gonna escort this young lady to the elevator and you fellas have a real swell time traveling," the cop said as he was leaving the bus.

Jug kissed Delilah and she, too, left the bus. He spent the next three hours delighting in telling his band mates of his escapades from the last two days.

By the time the bus carrying the Billy Eckstine Big Band pulled out of Memphis headed for St. Louis, the USS Iowa was pulling out of New Orleans bound for Philadelphia. Buzz and Bob were to report to Chief Papp in New York for their next assignment.

When the duo reported from weekend liberty, they never got the chance to see Caleb Stinson, since he was transported from the New Orleans police lockup straight to the brig on board the ship. Word around the ship was that all those caught at the party received a mandatory 30 days. Although they never saw Stinson again, the duo told all of his shipmates about what went on at the Saturday night fish fry.

For years, long after Bob moved to New York City, he couldn't resist going into a record store to check up on records by Gene Ammons and Louis Jordan. The Louis Jordan records stopped in the 1950s. But Bob could always find a Gene Ammons record to help him remember the man whose friends called him Jug.

*Inspired by the life of Baroness Pannonica de Koenigswarter and the
Mississippi adventures of Terry Spencer Hesser.*

'Round Midnight with the Ku Klux Klan

I f someone had told me two weeks ago that I would be on a train this
Sunday morning with all my worldly possessions that I can carry,
leaving Enterprise, Mississippi, and moving to New York City, I
would've laughed until my pudgy belly shook.

My daddy used to say that the Ku Klux Klan was going to change
the world. I never knew it would be my own personal world they would
be changing, but in this year of 1957, they have done just that. Or it could

Jake turned around to the catcher, then smiled and winked at me. "Sounds like the first bet of the year to me, Peter. What you say?"

"That's a good one, Jake," Peter responded. "Put me down for twenty big ones."

"Twenty dollars that Rufus Gardner, the fucking Fifth, makes the Ole Miss baseball team," an incredulous Asshole shot back. "Shit, I'll take that bet."

"What about twenty from me?" Jake asked, winking at me again.

"I'll take that too."

"What about a hundred from me, Asshole?"

Maybe it was the way Jake knowingly smiled or maybe I just sensed it could be my only chance ever to upstage and embarrass Hickey in front of his peers for a change. Whatever it was, it was the first time I called him my pet name to his face. He almost fell, rolling over laughing as he accepted my bet.

"If you think that's funny, what did you call him, Rufus, 'Asshole?'" Jake kidded. "I'll bet another hundred that he ends the year with a better batting average than you."

"Oh, that's rich," Hickey said with such a contagious laugh that I even snickered. "Ain't ya' gettin' a bit 'head of yourself, Jake? Let 'im make the team first."

When the coach came, he introduced his staff and the members of the team before taking groups out to the field. Before getting to the batting cages he took me aside and introduced me to my new training regimen.

"You," he said, smirking, looking towards another field, "go over there, run a lap, walk a lap, and don't stop until I tell you."

I wish I could have been there when Asshole heard the story of my tryout. I didn't because the coach kept me separated for two weeks where all I did was run, run, and run. Finally, when he let me practice with the team, I became the situational hitter. On the first day, the starting lineup was in the field and my job was to hit Jake's pitch anywhere the coach tells me. As I stepped into the batter box, Asshole started chattering at his shortstop position.

"Show me what you got, sissy."

"Hard liner to short," the coach said.

I could feel the muscles in my leg for the first time in my life as I took Jake's planted hard slider down the middle and tried to take Asshole's head off. The ball had no lift, but it surprised him as he scurried on one knee with his glove towards the ground. He got a glove on the ball but in an awkward position, then spun around and dropped the ball.

Jake the Yank laughed.

Jake the Yank and Peter, his seemingly inseparable friend, were my only salvation during my first year on the team. I didn't have much of a social life on campus anyway. Suzy Marks went to Auburn in Alabama instead of Ole Miss, so I made other female friends. Outside of a few professors and Diana and Jill, Jake the Yank was the only person I truly felt comfortable with. Why? I'll never know. We were complete opposites. I suspect I appealed to his ego by calling him "Jake the Yank," with his desire to be in New York overriding his Southern ethic. Who knew all these years later I, too, would have a desire to be in New York? Life is strange.

That year Jake the Yank was even better than his Southeastern Conference MVP the year before. But no matter who we played, the coach and every team member mentioned the loss to Vanderbilt the year before.

I usually sat at the far end of the bench with my head deep in my accounting book. Sometimes close to the end of the game, Coach would send Jake the Yank down to talk to me. He told me the coach wanted me to know the situation of the game in case he needed me.

It all seemed Greek to me, even more so if Jake the Yank was pitching, because then an assistant coach might come barking at me in a semi-hostile tone in a language I totally don't understand.

The bus rides were interminable, what with the noise and the constant badgering some of the athletes heaped on me. Jake the Yank and Peter always sat up front. They told me they sat behind the coaches to learn as much about baseball as possible. They treated the game like a science to study. Asshole and most of the others observed every minute detail of the games. I studied accounting, when I could concentrate.

Coach paid me no attention except to make me run when he didn't need me to hit during practice. When he did need me during games, he would dispatch Jake the Yank. That changed after the tenth game of the season. We had traveled to Nashville to play Vanderbilt. There was quite a bit of nervous energy on the bus ride. The squeaking, teasing, and playfulness of the players was unusually subdued. At one point the ride to Nashville before the game was more somber than the bus rides after games where the team lost. This game hadn't even been played. I noticed but I didn't care any way or another.

Jake the Yank was the starting pitcher. Before the game the team's mood was quite the opposite of the bus ride as everyone seemed more animated than usual. As the game progressed they were even more so. I didn't understand because every time I looked at the scoreboard between innings, neither team had scored. I also noticed that Jake the Yank sat by himself on the far end of the bench and no one talked to him, not even Peter. The game also moved along rather quickly. Before I knew it our half of the eighth inning had come and gone and not once did any coach come to talk to me.

Suddenly there was a loud pop of the bat that snapped me out of a hard equation in my book. The Vanderbilt crowd went wild simultaneously, and I looked up to see one of their players rounding the plate. He had hit a home run. In our dugout the second-string catcher threw his glove in the air in disgust and screamed, "There goes the no-hitter."

I didn't know or care to reason to figure out what that meant, but right after the comment Coach Mitchell ran out to talk to Jake the Yank and the Vanderbilt crowd booed loudly. He seemed upset and Coach obviously was trying to calm his star pitcher. I closed my book and watched an agitated Jake the Yank try to compose himself.

His first pitch to the next batter was a curve that even I could recognize from my disadvantaged view. The batter identified it also as he waited on it and he, too, hit the ball over the fence. Jake the Yank barked at the runner and the runner barked back. By the time he rounded third, Jake the Yank was beet red. Our dugout was quiet. Coach himself stood stone-like, while the next batter approaching the plate looked petrified. The Vanderbilt dugout, like the large crowd, was near riotous.

I started to enjoy the drama and for the very first time in my then 20 years, I was truly enjoying the game of baseball.

Jake the Yank threw a high fastball to the frightened batter who seemed to know it was coming. Jake the Yank took a deep breath and settled himself. He took another deep breath and threw a ball low and away. The batter swung and hit a soft ball in the air to our man at first base. I only knew it was called first base because in practice the coach would make me run there after I hit the ball. He told me that first base was all I had to know. Someone would then come and run for me.

My enjoyment of the unfolding drama ended when Jake the Yank came charging into the dugout making a beeline straight for me. Everyone else in the dugout was as stunned as I was. As he sat down next to me, he took a deep breath and I heard him under his next breath quickly count to ten. The coach walked slowly towards us just as the obviously tense Jake the Yank needed a few more seconds to calm himself to speak.

I remember thinking through those few seconds, *What the hell did I do?*

"Listen Rufus, I know you don't know what's going on, but I need your help here, so pay attention.

"I just pitched the game of my life," he continued, as I put my already closed book under the bench.

"You sure did, son," Coach Mitchell said, and as others began to gather around, he turned and snapped, "Gathers, it's your at-bat, take your time, stall, take the first pitch and stall some more."

"I want to beat these fuckers bad, excuse me Coach," Jake the Yank went on. "I made one stupid mistake then let my anger get to me and then I made another stupid mistake. It is only two to nothing. We can do this because you don't make mistakes."

Suddenly the coach darted onto the field as Jake the Yank continued.

"If anybody gets on base, my spot comes up in the order and I'll talk to the coach, but I want you to park one over that fence. I know you can do it."

Jake the Yank kept talking but I didn't hear anything he said. Suddenly I felt stress knowing I wouldn't be able to do what Jake the Yank was asking of me. I woke out of the trance by the round of boos that were raining from the Vanderbilt faithful. Floyd, the batter and one of Asshole Hickey's best friends on the team, was walking towards the first base.

The Vanderbilt coach jumped off their bench and out of the dugout to the mound and took their pitcher out of the game. The wait until the game resumed seemed to last an hour.

Our next batter hit the ball. I still don't know what happened except Floyd came back to the dugout cursing while the other guy was now at first base. As Peter walked to take the next at-bat, Jake the Yank jumped up from next to me.

"You get ready," he said. "I'm going to the on deck circle, but you're going to bat for me, and like a good ole boy, you're gonna hit one for me over the fence."

"Okay, Gardner, you get, get on deck and get ready to bat for Jake," the coach shouted.

"Coach," Jake the Yank interrupted, "let him sit and think about it. I'll get on deck."

Peter hit the first pitch almost over the fence. He and the other runner ran and ran but neither came back to the dugout. When they stopped running the coach ordered me to follow him as he charged out of the dugout running towards and screaming at the referee at the home plate. Exasperated, he told the guy that I would be batting for the pitcher before he looked back at me.

"Where's your bat?" he screamed to me.

"You told me to follow you. You didn't tell me to get a bat."

The referee laughed.

"Mercy," sighed the coach. "Go get a bat."

"This is going to be rich," I heard the referee say to the coach as I walked back to the dugout.

More than that, I heard people in the crowd laugh, snicker, and say things that were not nice. Asshole Hickey was standing in the on-deck area.

"Don't embarrass yourself," Asshole said to me. "You've embarrassed us enough in Enterprise, don't embarrass the whole state of Mississippi."

As if I didn't have enough pressure, Asshole made me feel every bead of sweat on my body. People in the crowd were pounding the insults, particularly about the way I walked to get to the area where I had to bat. I think I heard every individual word. It made me more self-conscious.

"Here's our number one," their catcher shouted to the pitcher, "their sacrificial lamb."

He was right. I was scared shitless. I was so hot I felt I was being cooked. I looked at the pitcher who had a smirk on his face as I put the bat to my shoulder. Then Coach Mitchell ran out of the dugout.

"My God, boy," he screamed. "You're on the wrong side of the plate. Look at the pitcher."

I had forgotten that I was supposed to look at the guy throwing the ball to see if he was right-handed or left-handed. Sure enough, when I looked out, this guy was left-handed which meant I was supposed to bat favoring my right side. I had heard both my father and the coach say I was a natural left-hander, which confused the shit out of me because I write with my right hand.

When I crossed the plate, for some reason it collected a roar of laughter from the crowd. I began to feel insulated. I wanted to swing hard at the first pitch just to have the hell of all of this over with. I saw the first pitch come and it was in the catcher's mitt by the time I swung. I had never seen a ball thrown that fast. The roaring laughter only dampened my spirits and made me even more nervous.

The next pitch changed my life.

I was starting to well up with tears when I put the bat on my shoulder. I saw the pitcher look at me with a menacing look and then a smile as he shook his head up and down. The ball came towards my head and I moved just in time, falling to the ground as the referee yelled, "Strike two."

Our coach went ballistic. The crowd went mad with delirium as the referee and the coach nearly came to blows screaming at each other nose to nose. I'd never seen two grown men so mad at each other. In my astonishment I hadn't noticed Asshole Hickey walking up next to me.

"Look at what you've done, sissy," he hissed as the referee was screaming.

"You're outta here," the fat man said to Coach Mitchell with an emphatic gesture, which only made him hotter. The other coaches came running out to try to restrain their boss.

"That's what you get for sending…" the referee paused and threw a look at me with so much disdain, it was painful to me, "…that thing to my plate."

He turned around and put his ass to the men retreating, pulled a whisk broom from his back pocket, bent over and swept off the home plate.

"Play ball."

"What would your daddy say now, sissy?" Asshole sneered at me.

Suddenly it was like time slowed down and everybody moved real slow with slurred speech. It seemed like an eternity, but it couldn't have been more than a few seconds. I looked at the pitcher and his face seemed contorted which made me feel sick. I looked back at the coach still being pulled back into the dugout by the other two coaches.

His mouth was moving slow, screaming at the referee, but the words were definitely from my father speaking loudly inside my head.

"If I throw at you high and inside, step back off the plate a step and pull the ball and guide the power."

It came back to me. He used to say it all the time, "Guide the power."

The sick bastard would throw close to my head and chest until I could stand back and hit the ball. Even after being hit and bleeding, he'd make me try again and again until I could hit what he called "hard high ones."

"Play ball, boy," the referee screamed.

He woke me out of a weird spell that I haven't experienced before that day or since. I've always looked at that moment as a turning point in my life that affected me positively for years. Only as I sit on this train being forced out of my home do I see the negative effect and how Asshole Hickey has hated me ever since.

"Yeah, come on," the pitcher yelled, "my girl's waiting."

I looked out at him and realized he wouldn't be throwing to the same person he threw his last pitch to. I walked to the plate with a purpose, and purposely went to the wrong side of the batter's box.

"You're batting the wrong way," came the exasperated screams from the dugout.

I ignored them and as I looked at Asshole Hickey, he was laughing.

"Hurry up, get this over with so I can win this game," Asshole said.

Everything slowed again like magic. I remembered at that moment that Daddy taught me to look for the ball as it left the pitcher's hand and to look for the direction of the spin. In this amazing moment I saw the ball spinning clearly towards me and towards my chest. I had plenty of time to step back and swing with a slight upswing.

It was the hardest I ever hit a ball and finally learned what Daddy meant when he used to say, "Find the sweet spot." I stood looking at the ball arc up, not hearing anyone in the dugout telling me to run. I did begin to run and stopped at first like the coach taught me to, but the coach told me to keep going.

"You hit a home run, boy," he said, while jumping up and down. "Touch all the bases."

The look on Asshole Hickey's face was pure evil even while all his friends were running up to me, congratulating me. They literally pulled me into the dugout, but I looked back to see that same scornful look. I always knew he didn't like me but now I realized that was the moment I turned into a sworn enemy.

After that my life at Ole Miss became much easier. I suddenly was invited to parties by campus social groups but never offered to join any. I preferred it that way as more and more people spoke to me instead of about me.

The baseball team left me alone to study and sometimes I'd listen to the coaches strategize and they seem to encourage my attention. I got a few more hits that year and next but none as big as that one. I beat Vandy which earned me a somewhat mystical status on campus. Everyone was at least hospitable to me except Asshole Hickey.

That was also the period in my life where I really learned how to drink. Considering Daddy's history as a moonshiner, I came to alcohol consumption late during a period where I couldn't pay for a drink at bar on campus. My last two years of college was also the period when my relationship with Daddy changed. That one swing of the bat opened up a soft side of my father that I'd never seen before.

It was my first lesson on how sports can transcend social barriers. When, later in life, Jake the Yank became State Senator Jacob Moreland, I learned how sports could transcend political barriers too.

Out of college I benefited too, as I was offered entrée into starting my banking career because board members of the bank were Ole Miss grads. I'd been on an upward trajectory at the bank since graduation, that is, until the night I heard Thelonious Monk. I've been trying to rationalize in my mind that since I heard Monk my life is still rising, just on a different path. In either case I never thought a black man could even begin to change my life, let alone totally disrupt it.

The flight from Enterprise that led the Ku Klux Klan to my door actually began two months ago in July on this very train to New York City. The owner of the bank, Royce Clarke, entrusted me to represent the bank at an investment conference that was being held in New York.

I was pretty liquored up after a late dinner, so I went walking through lower Manhattan. I was totally lost and wandering when I heard the weirdest yet sweetest music I'd ever heard in my life.

The place was called the Five Spot. I loved the piano and had always wanted to take lessons when I was a kid, but Daddy wouldn't have it. This guy playing the piano struck me to the core, so I inquired at the door.

"Who's that playing piano?" I asked the thin-looking, bearded young man standing there.

"That's Thelonious Monk," he answered, "and this is his very first week at the Five Spot. He's the new thing so you're really in luck."

I walked in and took a seat at the bar, totally mesmerized by the music. I looked around at the small crowd gathered and noticed there were black men and white men, some sitting together. I also saw a black man holding the hands of a white woman, something I had never seen in Mississippi or anywhere else. I was already intoxicated when the bartender talked me into a rum-based drink called a "Bahama Mama." He said I looked like I would enjoy that particular drink.

The additional alcohol did work through my bloodstream while my heart and my spirit were in the hands of this pianistic Pied Piper. I did enjoy the saxophone player as well, but my mind wandered whenever the drummer and the bass player played by themselves. It was a strange kind of music and I had no idea what it was or even that it had a name.

All I know is whenever Mr. Monk played, I was transfixed. At one point I felt myself swaying as if off the ground. Then the pianist got up and I knew it was time for him to let the others play without him.

This time, though, he began to dance. I was enthralled. Before I knew it, I was up off my stool dancing too. I had such a delightful dance with Mr. Monk, not that he noticed. Someone else did. His name was Jimmy.

I first saw him when I opened my eyes after my solo dance with Mr. Monk. He was sitting on the stool next to where I was sitting, and he had the biggest smile on his face. My first emotion was embarrassment. As I looked around, I felt myself blushing as suddenly I realized I had never been around so many black people in a social setting.

Jimmy didn't look like any black man I had ever met before. Certainly, no black man ever looked at me the way Jimmy did. My whole image of the Negro changed the second he looked at me. It was like a racial epiphany that I knew I would have to be careful of revealing in Enterprise. That thought made me blush more.

Jimmy was a writer and he knew so much about Negro history and the politics of the South. He told me I didn't know these things because, as he said, "It's the white man's story. That's why it's called his-story."

We talked all night from those bar stools until closing time. I didn't know what was happening to me then, but I didn't want the night to end. He told me all about this wonderful music called bebop and all the eclectic musicians involved. They had weird names like Dizzy, Bird, Miles and, of course, Thelonious Monk.

He found it fascinating that I would only let him talk to me when Monk wasn't playing. I absorbed every note of the piano and Jimmy's melodious voice. When the band began to pack up, I began to dread the end of the night. I suggested that we go back to the bar at my hotel for a nightcap and Jimmy laughed. He said it was funny because now, suddenly, I couldn't understand why his skin color would be a problem at my luxury hotel.

"What happened to the North being so much more progressive than the South?" I laughed in my drunken state.

Very seriously, he asked me to come to his apartment in a place called Alphabet City which he said was close by. The man was celebrating, he told me, as he had just two weeks ago received a monetary advance for his first novel. Jimmy was quite worldly and had success writing articles for magazines and industrial pamphlets.

I was quite taken with this Negro man, so much so that when he leaned down to kiss me, it seemed as natural as breathing. It was only my second kiss on the lips ever. My first was with little Suzy Marks. It was my reward for standing up to Asshole Hickey. I was repulsed by it and she seemed to be too. I had the totally opposite reaction with Jimmy all of these years later.

At 27, I could finally say I wasn't a virgin anymore. Not that I cared too much. I was always embarrassed by wet dreams and didn't touch myself like I heard so many guys talk about. I just really didn't think about sex until I met Jimmy. Now it is frequently the most dominant thought in my head.

The next day at the conference was a blur as I looked forward to another night at the Five Spot with Jimmy. I was so enamored that I purposely missed my Saturday evening train back to Enterprise. Sure enough, the second night was better than the first.

Jimmy took me walking throughout Greenwich Village, Soho, Little Italy, and the Wall Street area where the banking conference was held. My own personal safety was hardly my concern when I opened up a mail order account from a delightfully stocked music store that Jimmy said was his favorite. They had all the bebop musicians that Jimmy had introduced me to.

Since Jimmy had many of the same phonographs, I had the clerk pack them and ship the packages to Enterprise. When Jimmy played the music for me on his beautiful phonograph system, I knew I was not only smitten with Jimmy but this strange music he loved.

Our goodbye that Sunday afternoon was touching but not as hard as I thought it would be. Part of the reason for that was that I began to steel myself to the realities of my life in Mississippi. I realized and accepted that, after all these years, Asshole Hickey was right, I am a sissy.

I know I couldn't take the ostracism that would come along if that fact was public knowledge in Enterprise. That would be child's play compared with what would happen if word got out that I was with a Negro man.

So even before Jimmy woke up on our last morning together, I began planning a new life in Enterprise. Thanks to that black man, this white man found out who he was. Looking at him that morning I didn't want him, but I knew I now wanted a man in my life.

That Negro man opened up a whole new world for me. I was determined to make that world work in Enterprise.

That last Sunday with Jimmy was glorious. We made love again and he shocked me with another talent—his cooking skills. He was truly a renaissance man who seemed to know everything related to culture, politics, and American history.

After breakfast we took a walk to his favorite bookstore. It was a delightful, airy room packed with books both old and new. There were also records there and I found more music by all the music he raved about: Monk, Bird, Dizzy, and Bud. I loved those names and took notes on the songs that were playing on the store's record player.

When he excitedly came to me in a middle aisle with an early edition of *The Count of Monte Cristo* in his hands, I thought he was so adorable. He was so animated while he told me how the man who wrote it was a Negro.

That was when I innocently made the mistake of making an affectionate gesture towards Jimmy. I worsened that error by being totally condescending in insisting that couldn't be true since I once despised looking at Alexandre Dumas' portrait when I was forced to read *The Three Musketeers* during my third year of high school.

My innocent advance felt so natural, hardly anything that evoked the only anger I saw all weekend from that otherwise sweet, beautiful man.

After calming down, he explained some of the fine points of the hardships of being a sissy. He hated the word and compared it to being called a nigger.

"We just can't hold hands and kiss anywhere," he said, taking a deep breath.

"As far as that portrait," he said smugly. "That's his-story again, just what your white massers want you to believe. The man who wrote *The Three Musketeers, The Count of Monte Cristo,* and *The Man in the Iron Mask*, Alexandre Dumas, was indeed a black man."

This was all so new, almost surreal to me. I had never met a Negro who was offended by the word "nigger," or one who was so goddamn smart. Even when I was called a sissy, I truly never knew what the word meant until Jimmy revealed to me that I was indeed one.

Being called one before I knew what it was seemed wrong. Now that I knew, it didn't bother me. That bothered Jimmy quite a bit. He did mind the word. But what did that matter considering at that point I thought I would never see Jimmy again?

Once I was back home, everything was normal except that I kept thinking about what Jimmy said about the people I grew up with.

"There had to be more people like you," he said. "Think about it."

Think about it I did. The only possible candidates were two guys I met in high school through good old Suzy Marks.

One, Michael Stockton, is married to an overbearing, obese woman who moved to Enterprise from Jackson. It's like he totally submitted his personality to this obnoxious woman. No, he's not what Jimmy called a "homo," short for homosexual, one of many new words I learned from my black wordsmith.

I considered myself an educated and cultured person, but Jimmy gave me a different kind of education in a very short time. I'd say in a whole completely different way he's more educated and more cultured than I am. Jimmy has added a certain amount of freedom that I'll never attain. Life is funny: a Negro with more freedom than I have.

The other guy I introduced Jimmy to was Dennis Jarrett and he certainly wasn't free. He seems to be just as miserable as the other guy, Stockton. Jimmy told me that they're sad because for years they haven't been able to be who they are.

"You get good ole boy Dennis drunk, and I guarantee you'd get him in bed," he said.

When I countered that I frequently see him around the high school even though he has no kids, Jimmy changed his opinion about him.

"Oh, Dennis likes boys. He can't get any at home. He can't be himself, so he goes after boys who were like you in high school."

He laughed hard. "New dick," he said with sharp vulgarity.

In essence I considered the pickings poor in Enterprise. He cautioned me that I may have a hard life in a small Southern town. He suggested I consider a move to Jackson or Birmingham. He laughed again with that same taste of vulgarity.

"Maybe you can find you a black manservant to fuck there."

Surprising to me, even in retrospect, Jimmy and the whole sexual desire thing faded a little bit with me when I first got back to Enterprise. I thought less and less about Jimmy, Monk, New York City or any city.

Then one day as I drove up to the house, barn, and land that Daddy left me, a strange feeling came over me. I surveyed all before me, thought my life pretty good in Enterprise. That feeling was loneliness as I suddenly felt the only thing I didn't have was someone to share my pretty good life with.

The massive amount of land itself needs hardly any attention from me. Daddy left the management of sharecroppers to his old field hand, Benny. At the first of every month, the old Negro would find me and pay me what he collected. Sometimes when it is short he gives me a sob story about some hard-luck family that failed to pay all that's owed.

I suspect Benny has shaved some money and hasn't been completely honest and upfront with me since Daddy died. Ever since in my late teens I insisted on no longer referring to him as "Uncle Benny," his attitude towards me has been decidedly different.

When I was a boy Benny knew all of my many hiding places on the farm. There were so many tunnels and bunkers Daddy had used to store and hide his moonshine from the Revenue men. As his use for them lessened, I used many as a place to dream or read in the dark with a kerosene lamp. There were no neighbors nearby, so I learned to entertain myself. No matter where I hid, Benny knew where to find me.

He was good to me as a kid, so I begrudge him now if he wants to skim a few dollars. Certainly, after meeting Jimmy, I somewhat understand just a little better the plight of the modern Negro.

Maybe that's why on that day that I began to yearn for male company, the day Benny suddenly appeared at my door, I was kinder than I should have been.

Benny initially met me at my car as I pulled up to give me a package delivered by the mailman but was too large for the mailbox. When I saw it was all the music I'd ordered in New York, I was ecstatic.

I was so elated I rushed to open the door and invited Benny in. In fact, as I told him all about bebop, I instructed him to open the package. As he did, a look of astonishment came over his face.

"Why dis heah, aw all niggas, Misser, sir."

"Don't use that word, Benny," I gently admonished. I tried to explain the concept of black self-hatred that Jimmy said many Negroes in the South are accustomed to.

"So, yuh sayin' we's ain't niggas?" he replied.

"Do you even know what a nigger is, Benny?" I asked.

"Yea suh," he beamed, "it'z aw us down hear in Mis'sip."

I immediately saw the futility of that situation and switched gears by imploring him to continue to open the package. His eyes widened upon seeing Dizzy Gillespie leaning against a wall, ankles crossed with a red beret on his head, a pipe in his mouth, and his trumpet tucked under his arm.

Benny was transfixed. I had to push him to move on to other records. The next one was *Bird With Strings*, but Charlie Parker's picture wasn't on the cover.

"Bird wit st..."

"Strings," I assisted the semi-literate with his questioned look.

"Dis is a music of birds, Misser God'nah?"

"Of course not, Benny," I said, as he picked up the Bird record and there it was, Thelonious Monk, in my house.

"And this, Benny, is the most glorious music you've ever heard," I exclaimed, picking the phonographs up and rushing to my recently purchased phonograph machine.

I found three 78 rpm discs in the bound set as I hurriedly searched the titles looking for the song *Nutty*. I put the arm of the machine on the record and the melody instantly washed over me with the same euphoria I experienced the first night I ever heard Thelonious Monk.

The music was marvelous. I began to dance like Monk while

telling Benny about some of my great experiences in New York City, leaving out the obvious.

He looked at me quizzically. "Dat's the ugliest musik I ever her."

"Ugly!" I shouted, stopping the dance in my tracks. "You're not listening, Benny. If it's ugly to you, it has to be one ugly beauty. Don't you hear it, Uncle Benny?"

I didn't know where that came from, but he didn't react well. Looking quickly at the covers of Bud Powell and Miles Davis, he literally turned his nose up at them.

"I'se got wuk to do, Masser God'nah, whilest you lis'nin to dat…, whaevar dat iz. T'ain't music."

It was a week later when Toothless Donny Johnston, the bank guard, made his comment about the Klan coming to see me.

The thought nervously set in my stomach for days. How could anyone know about my sexual adventures in New York? I never once thought to think about my encounter with Benny until I was fighting for my life last night.

It is only now as I look back out of this train window and see the sun coming up over the horizon do I feel safe. Being on this train for hours and letting it all out in these pages already has given me a cathartic feeling. I know I'm going to be all right.

In fact, my life will be better in New York than Enterprise, Mississippi, because I'll get a higher-paying job. I'll find a man like me and right now, as strange as it seems, more than anything when I'm settled a bit, I want to hear Thelonious Monk.

Being settled is a far cry from last night. I wanted to relax with an early bath and my nightly Scotch in the upstairs bathroom. I was so excited about the impending weekend. I wanted to get an early start Saturday as I was going to spend the morning gardening and the afternoon listening to bebop while tackling some numbers in the bank's books. Sunday was to be my first day in weeks with no plans. I learned early in life that not only do I do nothing really well; I thoroughly enjoy doing absolutely nothing. I was excited.

I was laid back in the bathtub relieving myself sexually like Jimmy taught me while thinking about all the things he did to me. He told me that this would ease daily stress for me, and I found he was so right. He joked that my left hand could be my lover until I found a real one.

"Be sure he's as good as the hand," he joked, "or you won't

be happy."

I was chuckling at the thought when I heard the first car pull up, followed quickly by four to six more.

I reached for my robe and went to look out the bedroom bay windows and saw men with torches and other white-hooded men unloading the Ku Klux Klan standard cross, while yet another man was digging a hole.

Daddy may have been turning over in his grave, and I was in shock, especially when they took a torch to the giant crucifix and it lit up instantly. I was in a dazed awe, quickly dressing and watching the fire, not realizing I was in full view of the terrorizing mob outside my window.

"There's the sissy," a hood shouted. "Let's string him up like the common nigger lover he is."

I recognized it was Asshole Hickey by the way he said the word "nigger." And he led the charge towards my front door. Despite his costume, I knew it was Eugene Pherry, my office neighbor at the bank, running next to Hickey.

I quickly put on a pair of pants and ran to my Daddy's bedroom to the second compartment of his giant chest of drawers. The handle was actually a latch opening up a chute straight into the cellar. I jumped in and in a flash was whisked two stories below to the basement.

From down there I could hear the men frantically searching for me two stories above. I tried to stay calm, reasoning that eventually they would give up and leave.

I listened as they worked their way downstairs back to the living room, perplexed. I prayed they wouldn't think of climbing down to the cellar. If they did, I had my plan ready to get away. Daddy, in his prolific moonshining days, was very paranoid about the federal agents and built a labyrinth of tunnels between the house, the barn where the still was, and the woods out back.

I spent so many days and nights with nothing but a lamp pretending in the dark, muddy places. I thought of Benny always being able to find me and laughed at the thought of him leading the Klan to find me. Little did I know.

I heard the voices in the living room upstairs. It was definitely Asshole leading the charge. Then I heard Donny, the stupid bank guard, who couldn't even keep it a secret that he was bringing his friends over.

"Here's those phonograph records that nigger Benny told me about."

I didn't know the voice, but my first thought was I hoped that it was Thelonious Monk staring the racist back in his face. Then the thought of Benny chilled me, not only because of the betrayal but because of the irony of it all.

As the authoritative voice kept barking, I realized it was the sheriff. He was a mean son of a bitch. I had always heard the rumor that he replaced my Daddy as Grand Dragon of the Klan. That part of the rumor now seemed confirmed. As to whether Daddy was ever with the Klan, I could care less at that moment. I was just glad that he was a paranoid, sneaky guy.

I crept closer to my escape hatch. It was a giant washing bucket nailed to the floor. Even before I heard them turn the knob on the door in the kitchen that led down to the cellar, I lifted the handle of the big tub that had a trapdoor that led to a tunnel to the barn.

I ran the 40 yards, hunched over, and had a vision of Asshole teasing me as Coach Mitchell made me run at Ole Miss. The trapdoor was camouflaged above with an old large bundle of hay that was attached to the floor around other bales of hay. He used to have a large storage area built into other large bales of hay.

Just like his baseball tips saved me at a turning point in my life, now his ingenuity for always wanting a way out was actually saving my life. In either case, in an abstract way they're the same things: valuable lessons learned from my father. Only now, coming through this incredibly dangerous drama with life-changing consequences, do I understand lessons my daddy tried to teach me.

When I opened the door into the barn, I couldn't believe my eyes. There standing with a torch in one hand and a cigarette in the other was Dennis Jarrett. He gasped as he saw me coming from under a bale of hay.

"Rufus Gardner," he said, putting his hood back on.

"What are you doing here?" I asked.

"You're a sissy," he said.

Seemingly with Jimmy's voice I said loudly, "And you fuck high school boys."

He dropped his cigarette and started screaming and running out.

"He's in the barn. The sissy is in the barn."

"Hey Dennis, you even run away like a little boy."

I laughed feeling the spirit of Jimmy, remembering him pointing out to me men he thought were like us as we walked through Washington Square Park. I heard Monk playing one of those fast-dense numbers in my head. It was the fear settling back in.

That was the exact moment I found my way out and realized I had to get back to New York City, back to that man, Thelonious Monk.

I don't know how or why he should be on my mind at that moment, but it also hit me that Jimmy told me where Monk lived, 63rd and West End. I needed to get to 63rd and West End.

I ran across the barn to Daddy's incredible array of tools, now laying untouched, even by Benny. In front of the varieties of hammers was a giant anvil. It lay on a track that could be moved back revealing another underground tunnel. It led to the woods which led to the state highway into town.

As I climbed down into the tunnel, I decided not to bring a torch. I had run these little hideaways I found of my father's when I was a boy. I was sure I could navigate the way without leaving behind a kerosene trail like breadcrumbs in a fairy tale. I locked the anvil in place from below and decided to wait and listen before working my way to the woods.

Jarrett came in, shouting, "The sissy's in there! He's in there. He came from out of nowhere," I heard his voice get closer. "From out of that bale of hay."

"How come you didn't do something?"

It was the Asshole, always making his presence felt.

"I didn't know...the Sheriff said... don't do..."

"Well, I'll be damned," the crooked Sheriff said, in obvious disbelief at the magnificent work Daddy put into his fake bale of hay, tunnel, and chute.

Above the murmur I could hear the back gate to the barn being opened.

"He's not back here, boss."

"Fan out...get up to the rafters. You two boys stay back there make sure he don't make a run out to the forest," the Sheriff barked, firmly in control. "We've got the front covered. Look out in that forest," came the voice of Pherry.

"He couldn't have built a tunnel that far, boss..."

They obviously underestimated Rufus T. Gardner IV. He was paranoid as I grew up when liquor was legal. If he was the moonshine king he was purported to be, I'm sure he was super-paranoid during Prohibition. He had a myriad of escape routes, hideouts, and hiding places all on the house and farm property into the woods. I'm sure he and Benny probably had fake shacks where the colored sharecroppers live.

"Frances, you get out there, look what could look like a tunnel. Clint, you watch the along the driveway out front."

The Sheriff was actually sitting right on the anvil.

"This is the damndest thing," I heard someone say.

"Why Hickey, in his day, ole Rufus made a fortune moonshining.

I'd always wondered how the Revenuers never got to 'im. He was smart too. Old Rufus probably got hiding places all over this farm."

"Too bad his sissy ass son didn't get none of dem smarts," Asshole Hickey replied.

My contempt for him built up inside me until it was nearly bursting out of every nerve ending on my body.

"He ain't here, Sheriff," I recognized as the voice of one of the deputies.

"Wha'da hell?" said toothless Donny. "Whad'da we do now?"

"Let's smoke 'im out," Asshole Hickey said, scaring me so much I gasped and thought I was heard.

"We didn't come here to kill the man," the Sheriff said, coming to his senses momentarily.

"That ain't much of a man," Jarrett, of all people, chimed in pointedly with the others adding agreement.

"For all we know he could be back in the house," said the Sheriff, maybe remembering his job, trying to center this mob he was leading.

"I'll go check," Jarrett readily volunteered.

According to Jimmy, Jarrett is leading a double life. Here he's figured out how to deal with his sexuality despite how sick it is. It sickens me now to think how when I came home from New York I actually thought how it could have been different with Dennis, had we known. Jimmy was right; now I know I could never live in Enterprise, Mississippi.

"We don't want to kill him, Sheriff, just scare him," Asshole Hickey pleaded. "And if he don't make it...."

"Well, I could just tell Reverend Dale that it is one less homosexual in the world, which wouldn't make it a sin at all."

It wasn't so much that the Sheriff's compassion suddenly gave away that startled me, but his use of the word "homosexual."

"How in the hell does he know that word?" I remember thinking, incensed.

I had only heard the word once myself when Jimmy explained to me who I am. I was pissed. But Asshole had won and convinced his thuggish friends to go through with the arson. I started moving towards the woods. I didn't have to worry about being quiet as it sounded like a mini-riot four feet from where I was crawling. The last words above me appropriately came from my childhood nemesis.

"Don't burn the house. I'm gonna buy that beauty."

When I realized they were serious, my anger increased. The tears streaming down my face were only exceeded in swiftness by my pace to get to fresh air. I heard the hay burning and in an instant I smelled smoke.

Hurriedly, I made my way to the woods. By the time I peeked my head up under the fake tree stump, I could see the fire rapidly overtaking the barn. The arsonists had stationed two hooded hoods in the back so they could catch me running to the rear of the barn.

I put the lid down, climbed down the four steps Daddy built, and just sat down and cried. My eyes soon begin to burn as smoke worked its way through the tunnel. When I opened the stump for air, I saw the rear guards had left their post. I eased up the steps and sat in the grass with my legs folded under me and pondered what to do.

As the huge bonfire began to ebb, something strange started happening, very reminiscent of that day I had that big hit. I looked at my watch and saw that it was 11:50, almost midnight. Instantly I heard the beautiful Monk song '*Round Midnight* playing loudly in my head. The sound was surreal against the crackling of the fire, as if Monk was actually playing in my head. I closed my eyes and listened.

I clearly saw images. The first was Monk playing, but it wasn't at the Five Spot. He was taking a magnificent solo on the song and my mind's eye started focusing on his hands. His right hand did a long trill up the keyboard and then his hand literally flew off the keyboard and exploded into a shocking blast of white.

Then I was in New York City walking down the street with a very good-looking white man, then inside the lobby of a very large bank where another very good-looking white man walked towards me shouting, "Keep your freedom. Keep your freedom." The sound faded into Monk dancing and smiling. Thelonious Monk had shown me my future.

I came out of the vision with a renewed vigor. I could feel strength coursing through my body.

The barn was becoming a burnt shell and I could see clearly into the driveway leading into the road. The Klan had gone home.

I boldly got up, left the woods, and headed towards my destiny. I knew New York City was my destination. The thought began to consume me as I deliberated on everything I needed to do to get out of Enterprise.

The smell of the smoke stung my already swollen eyes and I began to wonder whether the fire chief was in on their Klan meeting, because there were no sirens to be heard. The only thing close to neighbors were the black sharecroppers who live clear on the other side of the cotton field, maybe a mile away. There were no phones there anyway. The thought of Benny being the cause of this saddened me.

The vandals left every light on in the house. That didn't matter as I left everything as it was downstairs, including leaving all the music. After all, I was headed to as much music as I wanted played by whom I wanted. The freedom was liberating as the song, *Well You Needn't*, came to mind. I whistled it while I rushed upstairs and packed the same two trunks I had at Ole Miss as quick as I could. All the while I thought of the legalities of the situation.

Getting my house was a pipe dream for Asshole. Prosecuting them would be impossible, but I've always had my business affairs in order since Daddy died and, more importantly, since Suzy Marks talked me into hiring her attorney, Millie Talnak. Being Jewish, she'll hate the Klan story, realize there's little we can do, and then she'll work overtime to help me liquidate Daddy's holdings in Enterprise.

While looking for some important papers, I came across one of Daddy's old guns. I took pride in the fact that I had never held a gun in my life, actually considered putting that fact on my tombstone. That possibility vanished after I opened the box it was in.

I stared at it, thought about how much time I needed to catch the 3 a.m. train to Atlanta, and worried about being spotted in my car by one of the Klansmen. I picked it up and put it in my pocket without once thinking about ruining my perfect record.

An hour later I was packed and had the luggage in the car. I had the nagging feeling I was forgetting something important, so I went back in the house. I couldn't remember what and thought maybe turning off all the lights caused that mental itch of "What was it?"

I bolted upstairs after completing the chore on the lower level. Upstairs, when turning off the lights in Daddy's bedroom, I heard a noise in the distance. At the front bay windows I saw the lights of an automobile coming down our private road.

I froze in panic, watching the car come closer. I shied away from the window to the edge as it approached. I didn't recognize the vehicle. The driver parked and out came the defrocked Asshole Hickey. Terror flushed my nervous system as he bounced with pep in his step towards the front door.

Running downstairs was out, especially since he headed right up them. I was too far from the chute, which they must've figured out and left open, so I tried to bury myself in the closet that was just this side of the bedroom entrance.

What the fuck does he want? I remembered thinking as I fumbled trying to close the door.

It creaked just as he was turning from the top of the stairs and made a beeline for Daddy's bedroom. I always thought it was a myth that people vomited or wet their pants in panic situations until that night. I almost lost total control and could feel the piss coming, then suddenly something steeled me.

I took a deep breath and heard the arrogant fucker enter the bedroom. He went right to the chute.

"Wow, how did that fat sissy even fit down there?" he said, as loudly as if someone was there to add to his insult.

I wanted him to die and it took only an instant to remember I had Daddy's gun in my pocket. I began to cry as I pulled it out, determined to get my revenge, repercussions be damned.

"You won't be resting in peace or hitting no home runs in hell, fat fuck in hell," he said, pulling out a bottle from under his shirt.

I opened the door slightly, held the gun and aimed it right at his back. Maybe because I didn't know what the hell I was doing and/or because I was scared witless, I closed my eyes before pulling the trigger.

He screamed. But nothing happened.

I opened my eyes and he was gone.

He had jumped down the chute. The gun had no bullets.

I tossed the gun and quickly headed down the stairs, not caring if he heard me. I knew there was no way he could beat me to my car. I had never driven so fast. That too was liberating.

From the moment the train left the Enterprise station, I've been thinking about my newfound freedom and exactly where I found it. I was emancipated by the music of Thelonious Monk. I'm going to rest and wake up in my brand-new home, New York City, where the past is history and bebop is the music of the future.

Inspired by one conversation with drummer Norman Connors and many talks with William Walden. Dedicated to Walter Beach and Richie Allen.

The Sidewinder

Sunday, September 6, 1964

Little Willie Malden was the first to notice the skinny little white boy as he stood behind the tree watching the band rehearse. It had been exactly a week since the Labor Day weekend race riot of 1964 disrupted Willie's perfect world of baseball and music.

According to his big brother Robert, white people were not only going to stop coming to their West Philadelphia neighborhood, but also stop showing up at Shibe Park. Willie couldn't imagine that because that's where his beloved Philadelphia Phillies played and at that moment they were the best baseball team in the world.

Up until the riots last week, the 12-year-old felt like pinching himself all summer. There was nothing he loved more than music and baseball, and Philly had the best of both of those worlds. The Phillies were winning every night and seemingly headed towards the National League pennant. Then, during the day, after he played many baseball innings himself, he got to watch the Lee Morgan Quintet practice.

The neighborhood was getting back to normal, but the little white boy hiding behind the big tree dressed in plaid knickerbockers holding a violin case seemed a bit out of place. None of the other boys surrounding Willie noticed, nor did anyone in the band. It was a normal Sunday afternoon in the empty field next to the DeBrest family home that doubled as a makeshift baseball diamond for the assembled youngsters.

The summer of 1964 was drier and cooler than normal in Philadelphia, and it was perfect weather to play baseball and music outside. The latter was the norm at this house every summer, no matter which jazz band James "Spanky" DeBrest was playing bass with. And Spanky had played with them all: Miles, Monk, Coltrane, Blakey, J.J., and his childhood friend Lee Morgan, who at this moment hit a high note and quickly brought it down an octave, shook his trumpet and made it growl at the little boys sitting under a giant oak tree next to the house.

The musicians and the kids were totally used to existing in each other's space, usually without interaction. The 26-year-old trumpeter noticed the week before the riots how when he played this new number of his, some of the kids stopped to listen. He remembered feeling he was glad he titled his album after the song. The record, *The Sidewinder*, had only been out a month but this week when all the boys stopped to listen to the band play it, Morgan sensed he had a hit. He growled again to tickle his miniature audience.

The boys again laughed. Willie looked to see the tree across the street hiding most of the white boy's body. The exposed head smiled from ear to ear showing he, too, was touched by Morgan's amusing musical statement.

For as long as he could remember, Willie always imagined that there was a young white boy living in an opposite parallel universe in another part of Philadelphia. That little white boy would be rich, of course. His older brother was closer to his age and would play ball with him and there was not a sister in sight. His father was always home at their big new clean house instead of always away working. Willie's world was the opposite of that.

That white kid got to hear the best rock 'n' roll records at night and got to see Johnny Callison and other Phillies ballplayers play pepper during the day. The 12-year-old reasoned his imaginary counterpart across town admiring outfielder Johnny Callison, the team's top white player. Willie's own allegiance belonged, now and forever, to the team's very first "real" black player, Richie Allen.

He reasoned that the Callison-loving kid and his brother who played ball with him lived in the Germantown part of the city and had a clean neighborhood that supported the Phillies. At his own house and with his friends, Willie was an outlier. His brother Bobby, every adult, and every kid he played with hated the Phillies. Even with the Brooklyn Dodgers who were now in Los Angeles, they were the team all his friends rooted for.

Willie thought about the kind of guy he purported his imaginary alter-Philly guy was. Then he looked at the shy and kind of goofy-looking white boy timidly peeping from behind the tree looking at the musicians. He knew that wasn't the imaginary kid.

What's he doing over here anyway? Willie thought to himself. There weren't that many white families left in that part of West Philly, and the ones he didn't know, his best friend Ray did. He was staring at the boy's plaid with disdain when he was shaken out of his daydream by the rest of the kids clapping. The song Lee Morgan was playing was over.

It was the sound of music that literally forced Shawn Berg off the bus as he rode home from his weekly violin lesson with Mr. Pisterman. The contrast of the young white kid in the black community even caused the bus driver to double-check. Shawn assured him the stop was correct.

Two weeks earlier, before the riot, Shawn had heard a clarion trumpet playing a haunting and bouncy melody that filled him up with a warm, joyous, and unforgettable sensation. Today when he heard the same horn and realized it was an actual musician and not just a loud phonograph record, he had to get off the bus and find the source. The civil unrest of a week ago was hardly on Shawn's mind as he exited the vehicle.

Rounding a corner, he was delighted to see five musicians in a yard playing music. It was a kind of music he had never heard before. The slender man playing the trumpet might as well have been the Pied Piper of Hamelin the way Shawn was drawn to him. He was totally oblivious to the group of black boys who have been playing baseball in the littered-strewn field adjacent to the yard featuring the band.

Those boys, like Shawn, were taken by the rhythm and melody of this particular song. Whenever the band played it, Willie Malden and his buddies usually paused from playing to listen. When Shawn did notice the boys, he was sure they hadn't seen him.

There was no way Shawn was going to keep looking at the boys. His plan was to just hear a little more of the music and hope the boys would go back to playing their baseball game. All he had to do was stand still behind the tree, then leave as stealthily as he'd arrived.

He felt his timing was good—the whole ensemble had stopped playing while the trumpeter just had the pianist and saxophonist play the melody over and over. He thought the boys would lose interest and go back to their game, but they, like Shawn, were totally taken with the musical line the band was playing.

The young violinist loved it so he began to wonder if music had some kind of mystical power. He reasoned, *Why else would he be standing hiding behind a tree in an all-black neighborhood a week after a major race riot?* He couldn't explain to himself why or how a simple melody had put him in this predicament. Shawn was scared shitless.

Had he the gumption to peek, Shawn might have seen that Willie was the only kid who noticed him. On this particular day, twelve of Willie's neighborhood friends showed up to play sandlot baseball. Had Shawn looked, he may have noticed the many varied hues of African-American skin tones among the baker's dozen of boys.

Willie, whose maternal great-grandmother was the product of a rape by a white man, had the lightest skin of all. The darkest skin belonged to George Knox, a chiseled, muscular preteen with a persistent scowl and aggressive personality to match. The two also happened to be fierce rivals.

While both boys were athletically built and tall for their age, they weren't the biggest in the crew. That would be a big, burly, hairy giant of a kid affectionately and appropriately known as Sheepdog. His kindness and ability to hit a ball a long way made him very popular among these kids.

Tank was the apropos name of Sheepdog's much younger and shorter brother. Had he the nerve to look, Shawn could have easily ascertained that they were brothers. What he couldn't see was that the older one had all the baseball ability. Tank couldn't hit a lick. However, the slight, short, little wisp of a youngster next to him always surprised the older, bigger guys on how well he could play the game. They used to call him Pipsqueak. It was shortened to Pips.

If Shawn had looked, he would've seen Pips as enchanted with the melody as he was. The little boy kept playing air drums while watching the trumpeter workshop the other musicians on his tune.

A blast of insecurity rushed over Shawn as he thought of the riots just one week ago. The trouble and real damage wasn't in the area; it was in North Philadelphia closer to where the Phillies played, Shibe Park. Still, Shawn tried to make his violin case disappear behind his body as he slid in behind the giant tree. As much as his mind was urging him to run away, he was overruled by his heart that was being totally seduced by the tune and the rhythm of Lee Morgan's trumpet.

Safely ensconced behind the tree, Shawn marveled at the slender, handsome black man bending notes that defied almost everything he was taught since he started playing violin seven years ago at the age of five. Since then his parents had taken him to many concerts, but he could never recall ever seeing anyone standing while playing the trumpet. He pondered the idea, questioning why the two men playing horns were not sitting in chairs when the words of his weird, mad, know-it-all uncle Neil rang in his head: *"The blacks can't do anything the right way."*

Were these men playing incorrectly? How could that be when the results were so pleasing?

Shawn debated these questions, internally remembering the promise he made to himself that he would never hate people he didn't know the way his uncle Neil did. He was particularly shocked when his mother's brother blamed the riots in Philadelphia on the Phillies' rookie third baseman, Richie Allen.

How ludicrous, Shawn thought at the time. The Phillies were in first place and Allen was practically assured the Rookie of the Year award. *Besides*, he pondered, *even though Shibe Park was in a black neighborhood, Shawn saw relatively few black fans at the games and none close enough to the dugout for Allen to shout orders to. He had to concentrate on the game, he reasoned, so no way he could help with the riots.*

His mind also drifted to the story he read about when Allen played for the Phillies' minor league team in Little Rock, Arkansas. He remembered being surprised to learn that Allen was the first black player in that town and appalled how the governor of the state, Orval Faubus, came to the game to call him names and throw things at the baseball player. He has never understood why white people, Jewish people, and black people couldn't get along. Most perplexing was why black people were so hated, and no adult had ever given him a good logical reason.

Listening to the bouncy melody being played by the five black men in front of him, Shawn was glad he came to see them. It didn't matter if the trumpet player's posture was correct or not, the notes he played sounded good to Shawn's ears and that is what mattered to him.

As the band finished the number, Shawn came out of his

comfort zone when the boys started applauding and headed back towards the field to finish their ball game. He took that as his cue to get back to Washington Street to catch the bus home. Just when he began to feel relief in not being seen, he heard the words that sent a cold wave of fear through him. He instantly knew that music had indeed gotten him into trouble.

"What that white boy doing behind the tree?"

Shawn tried not to look back as he walked away but he could feel someone coming. It was George Knox. The neighborhood bully looked so menacing and larger than life sprinting towards him that he never noticed another of the black kids right behind him. Willie was George's archnemesis. Willie knew there would be trouble so he trotted right after him.

As the other boys followed, Shawn became very frightened and fought the urge to run.

"Wha'cha doin' here, white boy?" the imposing George demanded to know.

"Leave him alone, George," came the order from Willie as he coasted into the scene.

"Kiss my ass, Willie," George shouted, without taking his eyes off of Shawn. "I will kick your butt after I dust this white boy's ass."

I'm not going to cry! I'm not going to cry! Crying shows weakness, thought Shawn, echoing the words from his uncle Neil after he was verbally harassed up by a bully at school.

"You're gonna have to deal with me first," Willie said, stepping in between Shawn and George.

This was a showdown that had been building all summer between the two boys.

"I ...was ... just wanted to hear where the music was coming from," whimpered Shawn.

"I just wanted to hear the music," George said, mockingly. "Well that's music for black people only and now I have to kick your ass for listening."

George lunged after Shawn, trying to reach around Willie. But Willie intercepted George with a two-handed push that landed the attacker on his bottom.

"BOOM!" came the collective taunt from the other boys gathered around. It wasn't until that reaction that Shawn even noticed that he was almost encircled by the other boys. He was looking away towards their tattered baseball field.

One boy, he noticed, a kid much smaller than the rest, stood outside the circle. It was Pips. He had his baseball cap completely covering his head with an oversized, dirty-white T-shirt that hung below his knees. The kid seemingly had no interest in the brutal beating Shawn was sure he was about to receive. He wanted to scream to Pips, *I'm not a white boy. I'm an outsider like you.*

George was fuming as he slowly picked himself up. Sweat was pouring off his glistening black skin. The sun reflected off of his flaring nostrils in such a way that Shawn thought he saw purple steam come out of George's nose. *I'm not going to cry.* But the optical illusion put such a fright into Shawn that he could no longer hold back the tears.

"Willie Malden! Ain't nobody did nothin' to you," George screamed, fighting back his own tears.

"And you ain't doin' nothin' to nobody," Willie responded.

Willie was the only preteen in the neighborhood that wasn't afraid of George. Though he was much thinner than the muscular tall bully, Willie was a much better athlete and George knew it. All summer long the two had come close to blows, mostly when the argument turned to baseball, specifically on the subject of which professional team was going to win the National League pennant.

With three weeks to go, the Philadelphia Phillies had a seemingly insurmountable six-game lead. That fact had hardly changed the dynamic of the main disagreement between Willie and George.

"Okay cry, baby white boy," George said, walking close to Willie while staring a hole through Shawn, who was trembling behind his protector.

"What team will win the National League," George asked, as he tried to maneuver past Willie.

When his guardian turned with the would-be killer, Shawn turned with Willie to keep himself wedged and out of reach of George.

"I'll even give you a clue, white boy," George continued. "It's the team with all the great black players, not the team with the one black rookie."

"You don't get it, George," said an obviously exasperated Willie. "I don't care how many black players are on a team, that don't mean that they will win."

George, Willie, and Shawn did a full 360-degree dance. Shawn noticed that the angrier George got, Willie grew calmer.

"He's going to make mincemeat out of both of us," thought Shawn, right before a sigh brought a flood of more tears.

"Well, what about it, crybaby?" George bellowed. "What about it?"

Shawn clutched his violin case against his chest and tried to contain the sniffles between his words.

"What about…" he sniffed. "What about what?"

Shawn hadn't heard the question or the all-important clue.

"What's the best team in the National League, honky," George again bellowed.

Baseball! He's talking baseball!, came the cool refreshing thought in Shawn's mind.

With his violin, preppie vest, and tie, Shawn hardly seemed the athletic type. The perception was true except for the fact that baseball was the only subject Shawn knew more about than music. He'd also been keeping tabs on the growing number of black ballplayers coming to the major league. Had Shawn heard George's clue, his rapid sharp mind still wouldn't have given George the answer he wanted.

By coincidence, the San Francisco Giants, the team with the most black players that Shawn admired, was in town that day. One of his favorite pitchers, Juan Marichal, was facing the Phillies at Shibe Park that very minute. The Giants would've been his answer.

Willie sensed the calm coming over Shawn and then said a quick prayer, hoping by some divine intervention that the white kid would say the St. Louis Cardinals, George's favorite team.

But Shawn never heard the clue. In that case the answer was a foregone conclusion. The Phillies were in first place by six games with only three weeks left in the season. His dropping blood pressure suddenly shot up as he panicked thinking of the race riots around the ballpark last week. In his mind ran the words of his mom telling him to skip his lessons and those of other adults blaming the riots on the Phillies' young rookie, Richie Allen. He panicked and began to bawl.

"The Phillies are going to win," he screamed through the tears, "and Richie Allen had nothing to do with the riots."

"Wrong answer, white boy," were the last words Shawn heard before George reached around Willie with a vicious right-hand hook.

Aiming for Shawn's left eye, some of the force of the punch was blunted by the late reaction of Willie. The blow eventually landed above his upper jawbone and part of his lower eye. Shawn had never felt pain like that. His world went dark as he let out a mighty yelp. Stars, lots of them, some yellow, some blue, flooded his mind's eye. Instinctively he fell down to the ground clutching his eye, oblivious to his violin or to the brutal fight going on just four feet away.

He didn't hear the cheers when Willie rolled on top of George and delivered a pair of fast, hard blows to George's face. The release of frustration on George's noggin was a thrill that the other boys were living through Willie vicariously. More than a few of them delivered blows in the air, enhancing their private beating of the bully.

George had grown stronger and meaner in the summer of 1964. Whenever the topic was baseball, whether it was playing it or conversing about it, George had definitely developed a major league chip on his shoulder. His mood over time wavered with the fate of the Cardinals, and they were having an up and down season. Like George at the moment, they were down—in fourth place; eight games back.

The rest of the cheering boys were happy. With their Dodgers long out of it, the Phillies about to wrap up the season in first place and, most importantly, Willie beating the shit out of George, all was right in the world with these young black boys from Philadelphia.

Shawn was just beginning to come out of his part-coma/part-fit when he felt a strong hand helping to lift him up. He opened his eyes and looked directly into the eyes of the tall trim man who played the trumpet. The boy felt the impulse to blush as the horn man's bouncy melody flooded his mind. Unconsciously he started to sing it.

"Tat-tat, tat-tat," he sang, hitting the width of the intervals perfectly. "Ta-da, tat-ta-da, ta-ta-ta ta, taaaa, tat, tat."

"Well I'll be damn," Lee Morgan said, laughing as he pulled Shawn up from the ground. "Hey dudes," he exclaimed, "the boy was singing the tune. Shit, if I get more white folks to sing it, I think I'll have myself a hit."

Shawn looked in the direction Morgan was talking and saw that the drummer had a bear hug on a steaming mad George while the saxophonist held Willie with considerably less effort.

"Yeah, but can he do the boogaloo?" asked the sax player.

As the trio laughed at the joke, Shawn noticed the kind face of the man holding Willie. He looked up at his new protector who was at the apex of a hearty laugh.

"Well, I know little Knox sure can," said the drummer to the men. Then, to a still struggling George, "Will you calm yourself down, boy?"

"What's this all about anyway?" the trumpet player asked.

"This white boy," George shouted, breaking away free of the hold, "came here starting things."

The adults quickly quieted the undecipherable din of thirteen little boys simultaneously shouting out their version of events.

"Whoa boys...one at a time," said the man with kind eyes. "It doesn't even matter who started this shit....I mean stuff. Fighting never solves anything."

"Joe is right, boys," the trumpeter added. "You shouldn't be..."

"He started it," blurted out Shawn while bursting into more tears. "He was mad because I didn't like his baseball team."

that would help the black baseball players. Now, through his uncle, he realized it applied to black football players too.

"On top of that, the uppity, ungrateful black nigger went on strike in training camp," Neil continued. "It wasn't because he wanted a raise. They already gave him that. No the nigger wanted more money for the rest of his nigger tribe on the team. And Mr. Modell had been so nice to him over the years," Neil opined, with a flick of his cigarette out the window on this warm early autumn afternoon.

"But..." Shawn tried to get in the fact Brown had led the league in rushing for six straight years. *That was something Brown did for the team owner, Art Modell,* Shawn wants to say. But his loquacious uncle took a breath and kept right on talking.

Well, he did get us into the playoffs, Shawn thought.

"Fucking niggers," his uncle screamed. "Don't forget, Shawnie boy; you've got to earn it."

Maybe they did earn it, was what he wanted to say.

"Who were the guys?" was what he managed to ask.

"Paul Warfield and Walter fucking Beach," Neil screamed. "Beach ain't shit and Warfield is a fucking nigger rookie."

"Paul Warfield was great last year for Ohio State," Shawn half-mumbled under his breath. He vowed to himself today to pay attention to the exploits of both players on this day.

"Walter Beach could use some incentive," Shawn bravely spoke up to say.

"Walter Beach could use a trade," Neil shot back chuckling, obviously pleased with his retort.

"You know who else could use a trade?" he continued, sharpening his attack on his young nephew. "Richie Allen, that's who. How's your Phillies doing?"

Shawn knew that Neil knew exactly how they're doing. He realized had he kept his mouth shut, he wouldn't have given him an opening so soon on their trip.

Shawn grimaced and tensed up.

"They're not going to make it, kid," Neil gleefully continued. "Your heart is in the wrong place. How many have they lost in a row," he snarled, "seven or is it eight?"

Six, Shawn thought.

At this point Shawn thought of reaching for the radio, but Neil didn't like classical music or the modern sounds that most people his age listened to. He preferred the older singers like Perry Como, Dean Martin, and Al Martino, all of whom to Shawn's taste sang mediocre songs. So the youngster tuned his uncle out until Neil realized Shawn wasn't listening.

He first thought about the great Broadway cast recordings his mom listened to. He stared aimlessly out of the window before turning to the only subject he ever saw his parents argue over, his uncle Neil.

Over the years he'd heard his father scream at his mother various epithets for Neil. A bum, a crook, a liar, a Jewish gangster, a bad example for Jewish boys everywhere were some of the lines he recalled coming out of his father's mouth. He's heard a lot more but realized the harsh words were never said to Neil's face, only to his mother.

He knew the reason for that was if his father did confront Neil, it would hurt his mom's feelings. Shawn knew that the last thing his father would do was purposely hurt his mother in any way.

When Neil thought he could get Shawn's attention again, he started in again. Just to get under his nephew's skin, Neil did a recap of the Phillies' current six-game skid.

The summary didn't bother Shawn at all because this very rational kid was anything but that when it came to baseball. The youngster had already decided that there was no way the Phillies were going to lose today because he wasn't going to listen to the game today. He was certain if he didn't hear the game that would be a guaranteed win for his team, because that is what happened the last time he heard a game on the radio.

From the time the car turned on 33rd Street and Shawn had his first sighting of Franklin Field, all thought of the Phillies actually left his mind. While the duo worked their way into the stadium and to their seats, the excitement of seeing his first NFL game with his favorite football team coursed through his body. He was so focused he didn't even notice the many fans in the seats listening to the Phillies' pre-game on transistor radios.

The pair arrived to their assigned area just as the players were being announced. The public address man begins with the starting offense for the visiting Cleveland Browns.

When Audrey Berg saw the usher point her son to the correct aisle, Shawn looked up and thought his mother's face was going to break because she was smiling so hard. He hurried through the six people in the row to reach her awaiting hug with his uncle right behind him.

He sparkled his eyes towards his dad while being smothered by his mother's embrace.

"Sure beats going to violin lessons, huh son?" David Berg asked, smiling to his only child while reaching for Shawn's nearest hand that was wrapped around his mother.

bench. Looking up, they could see the front lip of Franklin Field's famed upper deck, the first one ever built in the United States back in 1922.

"You folks come all the way from Cleveland just to watch the Browns lose?" a stout, deep-voiced man sitting a row back just to the right of the family asked.

Shawn was hoping no one would take the bait to answer the question. But, of course, his loud, loquacious uncle did.

"Nah, we actually live here in Philly," Neil started, before following with a thumbnail sketch of the family's history from Cleveland before moving to Philadelphia.

"Well, at least you guys get it honestly," says the stout man.

The man had two friends who were sitting directly behind Shawn and his mother. The trio were the only men in view who were wearing dress suits complete with ties. Shawn immediately took them for accountants.

"But why you bring Mommy with you?" another fan two rows up and left of Neil looked back to join in.

"Yeah, shouldn't she be home making humble pie for you boys when you get home?" asked the skinny accountant behind Shawn.

"Hell, she probably knows more about football than you do, sir," Neil continued, trying to give as much as he was getting from their raunchy seat neighbors.

It was right before kickoff when Shawn's hackles went up when the croaky voice guy with the radio made it personal.

"Well, who's the young fella's favorite player," the man asked.

Shawn literally felt his blood temperature rise after the old man intruded on his privacy. He looked to the left at Neil who was smiling just as hard as his mother was to his right. Then he leaned his head forward and gave what he hoped was a mean glare to his uncle.

But before he could answer, his mom chimed in. "I like the defensive back, Ross Fichtner," Mrs. Berg said, winking down at her son. "Ross Fichtner is my favorite."

In retrospect, Shawn realized later it wasn't because he was taking his mom's hint. Nor was he, obviously unlike his mother, worried about the crowd and their hostile attitude for Cleveland's marquee star.

It was looking into his uncle's disingenuous smiling eyes where his answer came from. He didn't answer "Jim Brown," the way 90% of every other Cleveland Browns fan at Franklin Field that day would have.

"Walter Beach is my favorite player," he said much louder than he intended, while still glaring at his uncle.

Neil, feeling the kid's disdain, impulsively turned fully to the man behind him and sniped Shawn's comment with an equal amount of contempt.

"I don't know why he would say that nigger when he didn't...."

Before he could finish the sentence, his mother wound up and gave her brother a full open-handed slap.

The loud crack silenced the crowd immediately surrounding the family. It was like a vacuum around a stadium of people getting louder and louder as the kickoff approached.

After a couple of beats, a voice from somewhere got a few chuckles saying, "Now that's why that woman is here."

"Don't you ever use that word ever in front of me or my child ever again," she warned in a strong, stern, sotto voce voice.

The referee's whistle blew and the Eagles' kicker Sam Baker kicked off to rookie kick returner Walter Roberts.

It was a moment etched into Shawn's psyche and replayed by the movie projector in his head for the rest of his life. There was more psychologically scarring film for a future screening on his subconscious to come.

A noticeable restraint evident in the home team's family section was aided by the fact that the Eagles' defense was absolutely flat, initially allowing Jim Brown and his Browns to move downfield.

Tension built from the first play—Jim Brown up the middle for six yards.

"Somebody better tackle that nig...Negro today or it's going to be a long one," the white-haired guy croaked, agitated.

"Did you hear how that boy Jim Brown joined up with that Negro singer, Sam Cooke, and that Malcolm X guy to not buy from white people?" Accountant Number 3 asked.

Shawn's ears perked up when Cooke's name was mentioned. He liked some of his music that he heard on the radio.

"Jim Brown up the middle for no gain," the stadium announcer blared, and the crowd cheered.

"I don't mean anything, but after joining up with those radicals, he should be banned from the NFL," the instigating old man said, making sure Mrs. Berg heard him.

"Yeah, didn't he say something last week about that Malcolm, X, Y, Z or whatever his name is?" the lead accountant added.

"What did he say?" the accountant in the middle asked.

"That he hated white people. The fucker calls us 'white devils,' when it's them who come from Africa?" the old man complained.

"That's what Sam Cooke said?" the middle accountant inquired,

143

looking for affirmation.

"No, Malcolm X said that. That nigger, along with Sam Cooke, Jim Brown, and Cassius Clay, want to make their own kind of money for their people," the old man continued.

"That's another uppity nigger, that Cassius Clay, changing his name to be a Muslim," the middle accountant said, totally disrespecting Mrs. Berg. "Like he's some kind of sand nigger."

"Yeah, ever since that Martin Luther guy started talking about the civil rights of the Negro, they've become more and more ungrateful," the lead accountant added.

"Just look at the way they tore up the neighborhood around Connie Mack with that riot a few weeks ago," he continued.

"I don't go to Phillies games anymore because of what those niggers did," the old man snapped, just as the football was being snapped.

Jim Brown then ran through the left guard and tackle for six more yards and a first down.

"Tackle that fucker, goddamnit," he shouted. "Sorry, kid," he directed to Shawn, "but they can't just let run him over them like last time."

The Cleveland Browns got the ball into the hands of the league's leading rusher four straight times for 15 yards.

"Yes they can, mister," Neil interjected, breaking the tension among the family slightly, "so you should pace yourself."

"Or you might lose your voice," Shawn's mom chimed in, earning a smile from her son.

"Do you believe they pay that black bastard 80,000 dollars a year, like he's some kind of god?" the old man kept complaining.

On second down, quarterback Frank Ryan faked a rush to fullback LeRoy Kelly, looked to his left, and threw a perfect spiral to Brown for another 13 yards.

"Yeah, I believe it," Neil retorted.

"The highest in the league for the best in the league," his sister backed him up.

Shawn hardly noticed the banter between his family and the four racists behind them. He had other issues as his focus was on the radio in the grouch's hand. With the Browns advancing, the crowd's disappointment was augmented by what was being reported through the magic of transistors as the Phillies were also getting off to a bad start.

The Milwaukee Braves' first two batters, Felipe Alou and Lee Maye, got on with a single and a double before Hank Aaron knocked them both in—for a 2-0 lead.

"They could really lose first place," the crotchety grouch groaned over his radio two rows back.

Shawn put his hands over his ears, screaming inside, *I wasn't supposed to be listening!*

The Browns are on the Eagles' 37-yard line when Ryan this time faked it to Brown. He looked to his left again for an instant where both his receivers were, before turning and rocketing a bullet down the right sideline that fell seemingly gently into the hands of halfback Ernie Green for a touchdown.

The quartet celebrated but it definitely was more subdued than it would've been had the family squabble not broken out. Many of the fans around them, including the white-haired man and the three accountants, pointedly booed at them after Green crossed the goal line.

It was the Eagles that made the section a little more comfortable when, after receiving the Browns' kickoff, the team immediately starts moving the ball from their own 22-yard line down the field. The long drive brought a sense of relative normalcy to the Eagles fans in the section, especially after Eagles running back Ollie Matson scored a touchdown from the one-yard line to tie the game at seven.

The home team had all the momentum even at the baseball game as the Phillies scored in the bottom of the first inning to make the game 2-1. On the football field the Eagles held the Browns to three downs and a punt and were just about to start their second possession.

As the two teams moved to the line of scrimmage, all the players on the field were suddenly startled by a very loud cheer from the crowd. The officials, players, and coaches all looked around, puzzled, as the lineman referee blew a whistle until they could make sure there was no emergency.

At Connie Mack Stadium the crowd of 20,569 exploded when the Phillies' second baseman Tony Taylor lashed a triple right after the catcher, Clay Dalrymple, hit a double to tie the score at two. The 40,000 or so at Franklin Field seven miles to the south reacted as excitedly. The growing roar and sustained shouting surprised a number of players down on the field.

The television audience had Jack Whitaker, the CBS play-by-play announcer, explain that there were baseball fans at the football game. But very few of the participants on the field of play or the officials, players, and coaches knew what was happening.

The head referee waited as the buzz reverberated around the stadium before he whistled for the clock to restart and the game to resume. But the collective charge from the audience was still too much for Eagles quarterback Norm Snead, who called a timeout.

Shawn's mood lightened a bit as he surveyed the field in a moment when some players seemed to wander bewildered, looking up at the crowd. That's when Shawn first noticed Number 49, Walter Beach.

Then it hit him that he had heard Beach's name last week when he was listening to WTAM, 1100 on the AM dial in Cleveland. The station had a powerful 50,000-watt signal, strong enough to reach Philadelphia. Beach had an interception and dropped it. He remembered it from a week ago because on the very next play, Fichtner, who his mom had mentioned earlier, did get an interception.

Now, looking down on the field, Beach took off his helmet, and to Shawn it seemed the player was looking up right at him. Shawn silently mouthed the words, "You're going to have a good game."

Beach lifted both hands in the air and with his index fingers pointed upward, seemingly communicating with his personal fan high up in the stands. It was a confirmation that relaxed Shawn even more. He thought about Johnny Callison and the Phillies, who were clinging to their 3-2 lead in the top of the third inning.

Number 49 then turned and patted the back and shook the hands of Fichtner, number 20.

The young sports fan was feeling good about his heroes at this moment knowing Jim Brown and Johnny Callison would come through. His new hero, Walter Beach, had just assured him even as the Eagles added a field goal to take the lead 10-7.

More affirmation came as the partisan crowd stood to acknowledge their team's lead. As one of the accountants stood, the sports section of the *Philadelphia Inquirer* fell to the ground out of his hand. Looking down, Shawn was astonished to see a picture of Callison with a cigar clutched between his teeth, smiling up at him.

The omen was actually an advertisement for the aptly named Phillies cigar brand. "Johnny Callison enjoys the good taste of a Phillies cigar," the ad read. Shawn could hardly believe it, following the paper up into the hands of accountant number three.

On the football field the Browns seemed incapable of any traction even as the caustic, sarcastic, and borderline racist remarks continued. The increased participation of the accountants was in direct parallel to the number of beers being consumed. The more the Browns' defensive line missed Ollie Matson running by, the nastier the comments got.

With the first half winding down, Snead, the Eagles QB, walked to the line, took the snap from his Pro Bowl center Jim Ringo, and fell back into a perfectly formed pocket. In an instant he saw his open man, tight end Pete Retzlaff, another Pro Bowler. He stepped up into the pocket and let heave a bullet of a ball.

In the instant he let it go, he saw Number 49 in his orange, brown, and white uniform running inside into his vision. Beach caught the ball in full stride, immediately reversed direction to the outside lines, and started heading up field.

Shawn was uncharacteristically beside himself. He stood up screaming, turned slightly to look directly at the old scruffy guy.

"That's Walter Beach," he crowed. "That's who he is. Number 49."

He kept shouting as Beach crossed the 20-yard line with only one man to beat. It was the player who threw the ball, the quarterback. Snead finally managed to tackle Beach at the three-yard line.

"I bet he won't throw the ball toward Walter Beach anymore," declared Shawn, continuing to unabashedly crow.

"Flag on the play," the P.A. guy boomed.

A shocked Shawn looked back up field just as the referee picked up his yellow flag indicating the penalty.

"It's holding on Cleveland," the announcer roared, crushing Shawn and the other family members. The home crowd cheered loudly as the officials confirmed that the play was nullified.

"Now I guess you'll sit your nigger-loving ass down," the mean old man said, with as much venom as he could muster.

Shawn whiplashed his head towards his mother looking for some protection. She looked left and back at the guy and gave him a vicious stare and sneer.

Despite his verbal abuse against black people, Neil loved his sister more than he could say. He just sat down after the play and hoped his sister would too.

The old man looked at her and rubbed his hands as if washing them. Mr. Berg was oblivious to it all as his attention was on the field of play.

The Eagles then played it conservatively, running the clock down before the half by rushing the ball a couple of more times. Their field goal kicker, Baker, then came out to boost the home team lead to 13-7.

The ball was barely through the uprights when Mrs. Berg got up, grabbed Shawn by the hand, and walked to the right past her husband. She walked the longer route just so she wouldn't have to see the old man who was sitting directly behind her brother, four seats away from the aisle on her left.

Amid most of the crowd rising to get refreshments or relieve themselves, Neil and Mr. Berg sat there motionless. The icy atmosphere froze them. It lingered after the kid and his mother, obviously pissed, left without a word.

Eventually, Neil turned to the four guys behind him and sized up the three nerdy office workers and the rude senior citizen. He then reached into his wallet and pulled out four crisp hundred-dollar bills.

"I don't know if any of you are betting men," Neil quizzed, leaning in towards them and making sure they saw the money.

"I will offer you ten to one odds that we will win this game."

"I'll take those odds," the middle accountant blurted out.

"What's your game here?" the gruff old man asked.

"This is an offer for all four of you," Neil said, as a quizzical Mr. Berg looked on.

"Oh, I got it already," said the lead accountant. "but how are you going to buy our right to free speech if we're winning."

"Well, no, we're going to win," Neil said assuredly. "If by chance the Eagles win I'll give you each a hundred dollars against your ten dollars if the Browns win.

"Here's your bonus," he continued. "You get to keep your ten if, and only if, when we get the lead, you don't say the word 'nigger' for the duration of the game. Your vow of silence can only be broken when your team is winning."

The fan to the left of the old man, who up until now hadn't said a word, perked up.

"I don't know those guys," he said, referring to the accountants. "But me and this grumpy load of coal here," he said, referring to the old man, "we have been season ticketholders for a few seasons now. Let me tell you, sitting next to Mr. Sunshine isn't always fun. And I've learned not to trust him as well."

He looked up at Neil from his seat.

"And I don't know you, so as a good neighbor I'm offering my service. Let me be the arbiter and hold the money." He continued, "If there's the slight chance that your team does get the lead, anytime that happens, I'll determine who crossed the line." He added, "I'm tired of all that racist shit anyway. People, it's 1964, for God's sake."

Not a word was spoken as Neil handed over the four crisp hundred-dollar bills. Mr. Berg looked on askance, obviously wondering about the source of the money. The quartet behind the family obliged, giving up their ten.

"That's easy money," said the lead accountant, rising from his seat. "Let's go get some snacks, boys."

The whole day had an arc to it that Shawn recognized as he walked the plaza of concession stands holding his mother's hand.

"Ma, I'm going to the boys' room," he said, after they had settled into a line and he was sure she had his order of a hot dog with everything, popcorn, and a Coke.

He couldn't explain why the thought of George Knox's menacing face occupied his mind at this time. As he did his duty, he looked around and it was only then that he noticed that there were no black people anywhere.

In a sudden rush, Shawn exited the washroom and did a 180-degree head-spin viewing of the milling crowd. He wondered, *Could the only Negroes in the whole stadium be down on the field playing?* When he saw his mother's face, it came to him from the depth of his unconscious.

"Willie Malden," he blurted out.

It was the name he couldn't remember but should have. It was Willie who'd saved his life. The name of the bully was etched into his psyche but until now he couldn't remember the name of the kid who was the nicest to him. That is, until now. *And he was a Phillies fan. He liked Richie Allen and George Knox was a Cardinals fan,* Shawn thought.

Shawn reasoned that he was led to these thoughts because he had made that mystical connection with Walter Beach. He wondered if Willie was thinking of him at this moment or hoping that his hero, Allen, would pull the Phillies through. Or would it be Callison?

A hope radiated through Shawn as he helped his mother back to the seats, gingerly carrying the four drinks in a tray. He was glad people had brought radios. This was going to be a win-win day for both of his teams.

Right before leading into the short tunnel that led into the seats, Audrey Berg paused. She looked along the concession corridor, seemingly searching. It was the same exercise her son had just worked through. She was hoping to see any black face to point to.

"Shawn," she said, squatting down to his level, gently putting down her bag of food and laying a hand on her only child's shoulder, "I've told you many times, my son, that no matter what, people are people. We're the same inside no matter where you go.

"I knew one day a test example of what I meant was going to happen," she continued. "I just always thought it would be me defending our own Jewish people, not Negroes."

It was at that point that Shawn had wondered about that word, "Negroes." *Why was it that he had thought of George and Willie as black, but he had never thought of Jim Brown or Richie Allen as black until very recently?*

He hardly heard any of his mom's speech of righteousness. Besides, he'd heard various iterations of the speech from her in the past. "Just be good to people and people will be good to you," was one of her many clichés. "Whatever good you put out will come back to you," was another, along with "God made us all one; we all bleed the same way."

However, he did realize now that his first NFL game, like the rest of 1964, was the continuation of the trend of race issues intruding into his life. The little fifth-grader was having a conscientious inner struggle with what race was in his world and the world around him.

Although Shawn felt it was more the other people in his life who were having the problem. He honestly had no hatred in his body and figured the only people he wasn't fond of were his uncle Neil and George Knox. Even then he thought he really didn't know George as a person. He was just scared of George, a fear that was palpable even though he'd probably never see him again in life.

"Ignore those men," his mom says, finishing her short soliloquy. "Now let's go uplift those Browns to beat these guys."

When they got back to their seats the four men were especially apologetic to the kid, particularly the old white-haired guy. It was hardly because of the wager or any half-time activities they may have missed. The four gentlemen along with countless others in the immediate area were, like Shawn, die-hard Phillies fans. Those alive before he was born had fond memories of the 1950 "Whiz Kids," the last group of Phillies to win the National League pennant.

"Sorry, kid," the croaky-throated racist said sincerely. "The Braves scored six runs in the top of the fourth."

All of the noise in the stadium whooshed out of Shawn's ears like a vacuum.

"The RBI by Felipe Alou was his third of the day and Hank Aaron's was his 94th, second on the Braves only to Joe Torre's 103," By Saam, the radio broadcaster, announced surreally, like a direct feed into Shawn's head.

"If they lose," Ashburn, the ex-ballplayer chimed in, as Shawn moved to his seat in a robotic state, "they will fall out of first place for the first time since July 16th."

"If they lose what will be their seventh game in a row," Campbell, the other announcer, continued, "it will indeed be the darkest seven days in Philadelphia Phillies history."

"Y'all, this game is hardly over," said an up-tempo Saam, in his folksy Texas drawl. "We're only in the bottom of the fourth inning and their pitcher, Tony Cloninger, hasn't been on the mound in a long time.

The score is eight to three and we've seen this team come from behind further than this. Let's see what the Phils can do."

The solemnity could be felt throughout the whole stadium. Radios seemed to drown out the building momentum of the start of the second half of the football game the fans were attending.

"Fuck the Phillies!" the head accountant exclaimed. "The Eagles get the kickoff and here, right now in front of us, we have a team. A real team."

"Yeah, not like those unlucky souls at Connie Mack," the middle accountant added, referring to the stadium where the baseball game was being played.

When the referee blew the whistle to start the second half, Shawn snapped back into reality.

Right away the Browns' defense looked like a different team. There were no missed tackles. The linebackers had continuous pressure on Sneed. Whatever head coach Blanton Collier had done to inspire his troops was immediately working, and Shawn and his family immediately noticed.

The better the Browns got, the worse both Philadelphia teams played. Across town, Dallas Green, the Phillies' dependable relief pitcher, was rocked for four more runs in the very next inning, making the score 12-3. The fans around the Berg family were soon to become more irritated with the Eagles.

On a third and three play from his own 35-yard line, Snead threw a long bomb down the left-side line. And just like his last pass of the first half, this one too found its way into the hands of Walter Beach.

"That's your boy," Shawn's football-loving mom screamed to him as she stood up to cheer.

The defensive player caught the ball on Cleveland's 24-yard line and ran it back 50 yards.

"Look at that **boy** go," the head accountant yelled, with enough emphasis that Neil couldn't have missed the meaning.

Suddenly people in the area were trying to shush everyone. Shawn was entranced watching Walter Beach celebrate after his big moment when he heard the tail-end of By Saam's home-run call on the radio. Johnny Callison, the first batter of the sixth inning, had just knocked the ball over the fence to make the score of the baseball game 10 to 4.

At the football game, on the very next play after the interception, Cleveland quarterback Frank Ryan tossed a 24-yarder to Warfield. Lou Groza kicked the extra point and just like that the Browns had the lead 14-13.

usually joyously celebrated.

Any day that Cassandra's friend Dione Larue came by was a happy day in the Malden household. While Dee Dee, as she was known, was his sister's friend, his father had had some kind of musical experience with her father in their youth.

She was the first singer Willie ever knew whom he could hear on the local R&B station, WDAS. She used the pseudonym Dee Dee Sharp and had a few local hit records. Willie's favorite was the song *Slow Twistin'* which she made with another neighborhood guy named Chubby Checker. He really didn't like her song *Mashed Potato Time* like everybody else did. Then again, he was really good at the slow twisting dance and never could really get the mashed potatoes down.

One day Dee Dee brought her boyfriend over to their house, a singer named Kenny Gamble who had signed a record contract with Columbia Records. Everybody really liked Kenny until in the middle of a lively conversation about music the subject turned to white people singing soul music. The two Roberts were obviously on opposite ends of the spectrum while Kenny, who like Robert Jr. had just turned 21, saw white folks singing his songs as a sure way to get his music heard.

To illustrate his point, he had Dee Dee pull out of her purse what he called a "test pressing" of a new single he'd written for a group that was populated with white and black musicians. The vinyl acetate that he had in his hand was like nothing Willie had ever seen before. It was seven inches like every other 45-rpm record, but there was only a little hole in the middle like, until now, he'd only seen on 12-inch albums. That fascinated the youngster.

He held it in his hand when Kenny gave it to him to put on the family's hi-fi system, another fascination for Willie. The label read *I'm Gonna Make You Love Me* on the top line and *Jay and the Techniques* on the second line. He put the needle to the record and everybody listened.

Willie had always believed that if Kenny had never mentioned that it was a mixed-race group, Bobby would've never known, and the worst argument Willie had ever witnessed between his father and brother never would've happened.

Plus Willie detected a little jealousy from Bobby that a guy his age was making records. Whatever the case this was, that day convinced him that his brother hated every white person on the planet.

Cassandra, her mother, and her guests were so embarrassed at the way the two got so heated about whether white people should be playing black music. Things only cooled down when Kenny managed to get a few words in edgewise and humored everyone by insisting that they listen to the opinion of the preteen in the room.

The tensions in the room eased when Willie responded by saying, "Well, you shouldn't have a man sing it, maybe a woman and man together, but not just a man. It don't matter if they're black or white; it's a great song."

"I'll think about that," Kenny said, before suggesting to Dee Dee and Cassandra that they should go.

"Spoken like a young man who appreciates Dr. King getting the Nobel Peace Prize."

"Oh, shit, why'd you have to say that?" Cassandra half-mumbled under her breath.

"Yeah, why'd you have to say that," immediately pounced Bobby. "That Uncle Tom ain't gonna do nothing for black folks."

"Let's go," Cassandra said, suddenly hurrying her friends out the door before kissing her mother. "Bye Daddy, bye Mom, I'll be home in time for dinner."

The door was barely closed before the elder Malden stoked the fire growing between him and his oldest son.

"Junior, you should keep your ignorant ideas to yourself when your sister has her friends over."

"Why, Sandra feels the same way I do," Bobby said, raising his voice.

"Look, I'm just going to go to my room because you two won't stop," Willie shouted, before running off to his room and slamming his door.

In addition to a spinet piano in their living room, Bobby had a deluxe toy model piano made by a company called Jaymar. His father bought it for him so he wouldn't play the big instrument in the middle of the night. The toy turned into an escape mechanism for Willie almost from the day he saw it.

He immediately retreated into his own world picking out the melody to the song *I'm Gonna Make You Love Me*, even though he'd heard it once. He'd just figured out the first line and thought to himself, *nice song.*

When Bobby came storming into the bedroom he shared with his little brother, he had a small suitcase in one hand and a ton of anger in his heart.

"Bobby, where you gonna go, baby?" Mrs. Malden pleaded to her son as she came into the room. "Put the suitcase down, Bobby. You and your daddy gonna kill each other."

"Nah, he ain't gonna kill me," he replied haphazardly, opening drawers and stuffing clothes into the bag.

"No, he won't have me around to kick," he continued, ranting while closing the case and going over to reach his hand around his little brother. "Be good, Willie. I'll be around."

"You ain't going nowhere," Willie declared, without lifting his head from the keyboard. "Like Mom said, you don't know where you're going."

Bobby didn't respond but sped by his mother in the doorway.

"Don't you worry, Willie," she assured, as she closed the door and blew a kiss to her youngest child. Little did he know that the next few minutes would be replayed by the movie projector in his head for the rest of his life.

Willie sat there working on the song when a lump appeared in his throat thinking about how much he would miss his older brother if he indeed left. The feeling was too overwhelming as the youngster got up and ran out of the room.

He arrived at the front door just in time to see his father knock the suitcase out of Bobby's hands. Bobby pushed his father away. The old man balanced himself, pulled back his right arm, and with dazzling speed planted a solid fist into his oldest son's stomach.

Mrs. Malden didn't know who screamed in pain the loudest, Bobby or Willie.

The younger one was in a state of shock and kept running through the door, down the stairs of their aging brownstone. Running on adrenaline, his intent was to run across the street to reach their family friends, the Victors.

Instead he ran right into the arms of Officer Gerard O'Malley, a mammoth, wily cop who was known throughout the neighborhood for his pleasant exterior when with a partner. And his viciousness and graft when he was patrolling the beat alone.

"Whoa, where you going, laddie?" the cop asked, as the thrust of the speedy kid meeting the man's trunk-like arms took Willie into the air a bit.

"Please come save my brother," were the first words he managed when he saw the uniform of the officer. "My father is going to kill him. Please come help."

Willie did an about-face but the cop couldn't keep up. When he reached the top of the stairs, he heard nothing on the other side of the door. He slowly opened the door that opened into the living room. He heard his brother's muffled cries before opening the door a bit more to see his father sitting head down, fists cuffed together on his mom's favorite oversize footstool.

Before he could open the door fully, it swung out with a thud powered by the hand of the exhausted Officer O'Malley.

"What the hell is going on up here," the cop demanded to know, barreling into the room.

"What the fuck are you doing up here," Bobby shouted, jumping up, forgetting the pain in his midsection.

"Bobby, watch your mouth," Willie's mom said, coming out of nowhere into his view.

"I can't believe you brought this pig up here," the outraged older brother raged, spewing down spit toward his young sibling.

"Bobby," the matriarch screamed at her son.

"Be careful, boy, you know you're still a suspect for throwing a Molotov cocktail in the riot."

This enraged Bobby who, as he charged, was intercepted by his mother.

The patriarch, who had wisely gathered his senses, quite calmly approached the policeman and chose his words carefully.

"What can I do for you, Officer?" he stood up to ask. "Certainly you didn't come up here to arrest my son for something that happened weeks ago, in North Philly. Besides," he said, walking towards the big burly man, "my son was home with me in West Philly the night that the Philadelphia police department decided to beat that woman. What was her name, Officer, uh... Odessa?"

"Bradford!" both brothers said at the same time, looking at each other the instant after.

The cop swiveled and threw them both a look before returning to the older Malden.

"Yeah, Bradford," he said defiantly to the cop.

"So get the hell out, pig," Bobby said, before his mom pushed him back down into the chair he was just crying in.

"Robert Allen Malden," she shouted, "sit there and don't say another word."

"I only came up here because the young fellow here screamed bloody murder was going on between you boys," he bellowed menacingly, taking a step towards the now-seated Bobby with his mother's hand on his shoulder standing above him.

"Besides, since they tore up the North Side we have to keep you West Philly niggers in line."

Without a beat, in less than an instant, Marjorie Jane Malden committed a crime for the first time in her life. The slap from her left hand was instinctive and so loud and so flush on O'Malley's right jaw that there was a slight ring of an echo.

"You're a peace officer. Don't you dare use that word in my house, in front of my son," she hissed, as Willie, the only person moving, pushed his mom away from the now red-skinned man.

The two Malden men were frozen, like time was standing still, as neither could hardly believe what they'd just seen. Their next instant depended a lot on how the officer would react. Deep down, each man did not want the tension to escalate, although the younger Robert Malden was more than ready.

An incredible number of dark ideas as to what to do next entered O'Malley's mind in a short amount of time. Fortunately, for all in the room, the aftermath of what happened when the aforementioned Odessa Bradford was dragged through a Philadelphia street came into the cop's mind.

He resisted the impulse to slap the woman who assaulted him, first staring a hole through her before looking down and settling his glare lower at her son.

Willie felt a chill go through him and he began to bawl, pushing his mother further away from the fuming man and closer to his brother's arms. Bobby opened his arms to his mother, looked down at his crying brother and back up at the now-smirking police officer.

Bobby knew what was next.

As if to acknowledge Bobby's thoughts, the cop winked at him, took a deep breath, and after a few seconds that felt like minutes, he turned to leave.

"If I have to come back up here tonight, it's going to be a lot rougher than the next time I see either of you..." He paused at the door and looked right into Mrs. Malden's eyes, sneering, "niggers on my beat."

The door slammed and the release in the room was palpable, evidenced by Bobby's mom unleashing a loud sigh as she reached for her heart and fell back into his arms. Willie ran to the door and shushed everyone as he listened for the door to close at the bottom of the flight of stairs.

"Wow, Dad, Mom," he released, running into the arms of his dad. "I didn't even know you knew who Odessa Bradford was."

"Me, either," Bobby agreed, smiling at his father and simultaneously letting go of the anger he was feeling toward him while hugging his mother even tighter.

"And Mom, what got into you?"

The normally shy woman blushed, put her head in her son's

chest. "I guess I just instinctively had to protect my guys."

"Well, your instinct almost got us all put in the clink," he said, laughing, "including Willie."

"Yeah, 'cause he was gonna go down," Willie said, with a sense of pride.

"Now I want you, Bobby, to take the suitcase, get these clothes and put them away," she said, pushing her son away. "I'll go talk to your father."

The minds of both Willie and Bobby were flooded with adrenaline, replaying the last few minutes that became lore in their neighborhood.

Both of them couldn't wait to tell Cassandra.

Sunday, October 10, 1965

This was a day Shawn had all to himself to decide what he wanted to do. He was going to watch the third game of the World Series on television with his father and uncle. Instead he decided to close his bedroom door and take the positive energy from the day before and devote it to music.

On this day Shawn was feeling like a champion. Yesterday he attended his second NFL game. This time it was a Saturday afternoon game in Cleveland, the game where the Browns received their championship rings. The Phillies may have imploded in spectacularly historic fashion in 1964; his favorite football team, on the other hand, went all the way.

His depression over how the baseball home team faltered was immense. But every weekend Jim Brown, Walter Beach, Frank Ryan, Paul Warfield, Ross Fichtner, Gary Collins, Lou Groza, and the rest of the Cleveland Browns made him feel better. They eventually won the Eastern Division title with a record of 10-3-1.

His emotional high reached a fever pitch at the end of the year when on December 27th, for the first time ever, the NFL title game was televised nationally. Eighty thousand people were at Cleveland's Municipal Stadium to see the vaunted Baltimore Colts, led by second-year coach Don Shula. With their league-leading high-powered offense, they were heavily favored to win the game.

But the Berg family watched on CBS as their heroes on defense stifled quarterback Johnny Unitas, and Gary Collins scored a league-record three touchdowns. Each catch eased the pain Shawn felt when Callison's three home runs couldn't deliver the Phillies on the day of his first NFL game. Unitas may have stopped Brown from winning his third MVP title in 1964, but number 32's team embarrassed the Colts 27-0.

On that last Sunday in 1964, the Browns' victory felt like he had exacted a bit of revenge on George Knox. Shawn still had trouble remembering the name of the kid who saved him or any of the musicians, but not George. What stood out to him was that melody the trumpeter played and the hurt, both physical and psychological, dealt to him by the young black boy that fateful day.

Shawn was a champion in 1964 with his football team the Browns, just like George was a champion with the baseball Cardinals. CBS was into the post-game interviews on the television when he was thinking to himself how he never thought of Walter Beach or Jim Brown as black, the way he thought about George. He was daydreaming with those thoughts when his mother woke him out of it.

"How 'bout we go to a game, Shawnie," she beamed.

"Mom, this championship game is over," he laughed.

"No, not this game, silly," she laughed with him. "Next year."

"That's a great idea," his pop exalted from the opposite twin rocker that his mom was sitting in, across from the new Christmas-gifted television set.

The championship win brought race to mind that December day for Shawn because of his experience with the young black kids and the mean men he met at his first NFL game. Plus, just two weeks earlier, he heard that Sam Cooke was murdered. That day, December 11th, also made Shawn think of where he stood on the topic of black people and the nasty things that were said about the singer by the quartet of shitty white people he met at his first Browns game.

The second time he saw his defending champion Cleveland Browns up their record to 3 and 1 by beating the Pittsburgh Steelers 24-19. He was there at Municipal Stadium in Cleveland last night to see it, and on this Sunday, in Philadelphia all was right with the world.

He had no idea how, on the day after his second NFL game, all those feelings from those two experiences would collide with his love of music, and come rushing to the forefront. Every emotion he felt that day he met George Knox and that he experienced at the Eagles football game would soon be boiling over again.

Shawn paid no attention to the one-year anniversary of his altercation with George. As far as baseball was concerned, 1965 was a totally different year for fans of the Phillies and the Cardinals. Shawn's team, the Phillies, finished in sixth place.

Johnny Callison not only hit his usual 30-plus homers but also for the second time in his career led the league in triples. Bunning matched his 29 wins from the near-miss year but the rest of the team didn't jell.

It was Allen who had led the league in triples and runs the year before when he was named National League Rookie of the Year. He actually had a great sophomore year, but with oversize expectations on his shoulder, the young black player took a lot of heat for his 20 homers/81 RBI/93 runs/.302 batting average season.

The only reason he didn't lead the league in triples in '65 was that his teammate Callison, like in '64, sizzled the whole year. It was rumored that manager Gene Mauch and Allen feuded, which in Shawn's opinion fueled the bad press and bad-mouthing the black player received from his own friends and especially Uncle Neil.

All summer long as the team faded, Shawn thought about last season sitting at that football game and wondered if white people in Philadelphia didn't like Richie Allen just because he was one of the team's very few black players.

On the other hand, the young man questioned his obsession with watching the progress of George Knox's St. Louis Cardinals all season. He reasoned that he wasn't racist every day as he checked their progress and found joy every time they lost, which they did plenty. In Shawn's mind's eye, each loss was an imaginary punch to Knox's noggin.

Midseason, when it was obvious neither team would find traction, besting St. Louis was all that mattered. He found so much satisfaction that George's team finished the year in seventh place. They lost more than they won, only besting the woebegotten Chicago Cubs and the two expansion teams—the New York Mets and the Houston Colts, who in 1965 moved into their new artificial-turf stadium, the Astrodome, and changed their name to the Astros.

The Berg family listened to the World Series the day before at the start of their seven-hour journey home after the football game in Cleveland. The National League champion was the Los Angeles Dodgers. Their opponent was the American League champion Minnesota Twins. Because the baseball game was played on the West Coast, it was just starting on the radio by the time the Browns football game was over and the family got to their car at Municipal Stadium.

Heading east to Philly, Shawn heard most of what was the third game of the series, which the Twins led 2-0. He was really surprised that the announcer for the game was By Saam, the same guy who was worked for the Phillies. But his on-air partner was a guy named Joe Garagiola. It felt traitorous to the young Phillies fan.

His parents tried to explain to him that it was for a national audience, much like the Browns' championship game was for everyone.

"By is just doing his job," his mother reassured him, as she turned from the front seat of the car to hand him a sandwich. "He can't be on anybody's side when he's on the radio talking about a championship game."

Ever since that first-ever broadcast of an NFL championship game and the death of Sam Cooke last December, Shawn had been learning and feeling that the world was so much bigger than Philadelphia and Cleveland. That feeling returned when his father and uncle, who was in the back seat with him, got into a lengthy argument over whether it was right for star Dodgers pitcher Sandy Koufax to not pitch in Game 1 because it fell on Yom Kippur.

He remembered falling asleep thinking, *Wait, did we celebrate Yom Kippur this year?* The sixth-grader woke up being pulled to his bed after the long drive. The Dodgers won Game 3, four-zip behind Claude Olsteen. Since Shawn didn't really care who won, and the star Dodger pitcher Koufax wasn't pitching that day, he declined the offer from his father to watch Game 4 later that afternoon on television.

The violin excited Shawn like never before, and he couldn't wait to spend the day rehearsing and practicing. He fell asleep the night before with repeated phrases of the *The Sidewinder* in his head. The young musician had used the riff as a warm-up exercise so much he learned it in ten different keys and after time embellished on the simple melody.

There were other reasons for Shawn's newfound excitement over his instrument, chief among them being a girl.

Her name was Ora Jean Whu. She had also contributed to Shawn's growing sense of the bigger world and his place in it. He met her at the city's summer music camp for gifted students. It was through the Philadelphia Youth Orchestra that he met a new private teacher, eliminating both the lessons with Mr. Pisterman and the long bus ride through a black neighborhood.

And it was through the PYO that he met his first love.

She was thin and a bit taller than Shawn with long straight black hair that parted evenly down each side of her broad bony shoulders. She had a very attractive, almost exotic face that gave only a small hint of the Asian heritage her name suggested. Ora Jean was the first violin player he'd met in his age group who was obviously better than him. He wasn't sure if that was the reason she intimidated him.

Even though they sat two seats away from each other in the violin section twice a week all summer, he barely said a word to her. She hardly said a word to anyone through rehearsals, including the instructor, even though she was first violinist in the section. Ora said less to him and he was totally smitten.

After the All-City High School Orchestra Labor Day Weekend Concert, he wondered if he would ever see Ora again.

Then on the first day of sixth grade on the playground of the new middle school, there she was with four other girls. She seemed like a totally different human, laughing and being goofy with friends who were obviously funneled together from another neighborhood grammar school.

He froze when he saw her, and she smiled and gave a happy little wave. The boy beat himself up that whole first day for only being able to emit a slight smirk and a tiny wave she probably didn't see. She may not have been a really shy person but he certainly was.

Ora didn't think much of that playground encounter but thought about Shawn plenty when she noticed later in the week a flyer asking for applications for the fall Columbus Day talent show. When she showed up in his Social Studies & Civics class and he seemingly didn't react, Ora thought Shawn didn't like her.

That changed a week later when for two days that class had to read out loud the first assignment of the year: "What Was the Most Important Thing I Learned This Summer." The teacher, Mr. Gordon, decided to start in reverse order of the alphabet, which after Susan Williams made Ora Jane Whu second.

"Over the summer I learned about the Immigration Act of 1965," the pretty girl started confidently in front of the class. "I learned that my ancestors used to not be allowed in the United States.

"This summer I learned my father was in a Japanese prison camp in California even though he is Chinese," she added, dramatically leaving her classmates tantalized, especially Shawn.

As she spoke he could feel his body temperature surge. This was not the same girl he played violin with this summer. Even on the playground he noticed she had a different demeanor than she did when they played music together with the PYO.

"I learned that through the Immigration Act of 1965, that kind of thing could never happen to someone like my father ever again."

Shawn was spellbound, so much so that he could feel that he was blushing. He was only sitting three rows from the front, near the center of the room. He was getting warm and thought it best to divert his eyes in case she noticed. This bout of insecurity subsided quickly when he looked around the classroom to see Ora Jane also had the intense rapt attention of his classmates as well.

When he looked back up at her, for the first time in his life he wondered how does love feel? After she cited some similarities with the Civil Rights Act of 1964 in her next paragraph, he somehow knew he was in love. He also knew that he could and would never tell her that.

She went on to explain how the bill was just passed by the House of Representatives last month and was sure to pass the Senate next week. While listening and adoring her, he still couldn't shake the feeling that she was noticing him.

The more she continued the more he tried to keep stern and act nonchalant, but was sure his act wasn't working.

"After it passes, people like my dad and me will never be discriminated against again. It will be the law," she finished, flourishing her last words with a sense of pride.

As she strolled to her seat serenaded by enthusiastic applause from her peers, Shawn was now wishing he sat behind her instead of the other way around. With Ora Jane at the back of the room he became even more self-conscious and nervous. He wondered if she was looking at him and if so, what she was thinking?

The kid didn't even really hear the other speeches. Instead he used the time to muscle up the courage to compliment her on her terrific speech after the class was over. But he knew he couldn't do it.

He began to lament that he had no older sibling to talk to for advice. He cursed the junior high school for having a band instead of an orchestra. Will he have to wait until next summer to talk to her, he thought?

That's ridiculous, he almost voiced while Abagail Schumann discussed the dimensions of the Empire State Building in New York City.

I'm going to stand up to her, he thought. *I'm going to say, "Ora Jean, I really liked your speech. And I really like your violin playing too."*

It seemed forever before Mr. Gordon dismissed the class with a reminder for the remainder of the class to be ready with their presentations the next day. He stood and took a deep breath as he gathered his belongings. Turning, he saw not only Ora Jane's friends rush her, but also a couple of the athletic types who intimidated him on the playground.

She's going to be the popular cheerleader type, he thought, as symbolically a piece of paper fell from his books. It was his staunch resolution withering away. He left the room and sulked all the way to his locker.

"Hey, Shawn Berg," came a loud voice from the other side of the locker door.

He turned in the crowded hallway to see Ora Jane coming at him with a piece of paper in her hand.

"Shawn Berg, have you seen this," she asked, repeating his name rapidly as if it was one word.

In her hand was a freshly mimeographed, barely dry copy of the details of the fall talent show on Monday, October 11.

"We could win this, Shawn Berg," she almost commanded, walking up to him.

"I will write music for us to play," she continued. "All you have to do is meet me in the music room tomorrow after school. Is that okay, Shawn Berg?"

"Yes," he said, in a soft-spoken voice.

She did an immediate U-turn and quickly walked away.

"Hey," he said, speaking up. "Why do you call me Shawn Berg like that?"

"Because I can tell that you don't like me, Shawn Berg?"

"I...I...I do like you," was all he could muster for a beat.

For a moment he couldn't think or breathe.

"I...I did, I mean I do like you," the words now coming out of his mouth without the advantage of thought.

"...I mean your speech, your skirt, and the way you play violin."

Actually Ora Jane did notice that she had Shawn's total attention when she was speaking. He was right to wonder if she was looking at him. She was looking way beyond the jocks to look for his reaction after she was seated. And she was really miffed when he hadn't come and congratulated her after class.

"Well, how come you didn't say so, Shawn Berg?"

"I...I...I"

"Be there tomorrow after school, Shawn Berg, and we won't be playing Mozart and Beethoven," she said, twisting and turning to walk away as the crowd around them began to thin.

Then she turned, gave a big smile that melted Shawn's heart, and walked back up to him to almost whisper her next words.

"We're going to playing Sam Cooke," she said, turning again.

"You know who Sam Cooke is?" he asked, stopping her cold.

"You know who Sam Cooke is?" she inquired, with almost a hint of not believing that he did know anything about the singer.

He just gave her a look of assurance.

"Do you know who Art Fleming is?" she asked, as if a dare.

"You watched *Jeopardy*," he mocked incredulously, speaking of the host of the year-old game show that was gaining popularity.

"Do you know who George Harrison is?" she countered.

become a complete musician. But they were talking about Mozart with a full orchestra, not the music of Sam Cooke being played by a beautiful Asian woman whistling and playing cello.

Their first run through the song was mesmerizing for the young man. The magical moments were underscored when for the first time Ora Jane looked him directly in his eyes and complimented him using only his given name.

"That was wonderful, Shawn," she almost whispered.

It would take them a half dozen more tries before they could play it as well as they played it the first time. Afterwards they talked for an hour.

She told him how she discovered Sam Cooke. Her mother had the long-playing album *The Best of Sam Cooke*. She described the bright yellow background of the album's cover and the bright red font stating the title.

"And he's so handsome," she cooed.

He then told her his weird Sam Cooke story and how he discovered him from racist people who didn't like his politics. He paused after visibly upsetting her with news of his death and how he died. She hadn't known.

Shawn only found out because he avidly read the daily *Philadelphia Inquirer's* sports section. The inner portion where the sports section starts is across from where the obituaries begin. He bought a few of his 45 singles after his encounter with the racists last year at the football game. He bought two more when he heard he died in December.

"The one I like most is called *Another Saturday Night*," Shawn exclaimed.

"Then we must play that too at the talent show," she declared.

That was more than three weeks ago and the talent show was now a day away. That's why Shawn wanted to just practice and not watch the World Series at all.

Since that time the two met a few more times to play the music and go over some ideas Ora Jane had to spice up their presentation. She had no intention of saving all the spice for the music.

They crossed the puppy love Rubicon at a local ice cream shop the weekend before. She tried to be as open as she could that day. She told him how she'd lived in Northern California for five years, New York City for almost as much time, and Philadelphia for just three.

He found her aggressive, talkative, adaptive to change, and open to strangers, all qualities he felt he lacked. More than anything, he found her beautiful. To him she was an obviously worldly young lady who was way wiser than her thirteen years might suggest.

Ora Jane was full of surprises and Shawn loved them all. He'd never met anyone as passionate or with as much willpower. She changed his life in more ways than one when they went for a walk in a park after sharing a huge banana split.

Sitting on a bench in the park a week before, he had learned that she'd only become a musician because her mom wanted her to do girlie things like ballet, model, cook, and shop for clothes.

"She wanted me to play with Barbie dolls and wanted me to have one of those new Easy Bake Ovens," Ora Jane explained.

"It was my dad who said to me, 'If you get good at music, your mother will leave you alone.' It was a ploy on his part and it worked," she continued. "He loves music and now so do I. I love nothing more."

Ora Jane was proficient at piano by seven, learned the violin by ten.

"The cello was just something I picked up on the way," she said, almost embarrassed by her riches.

He learned that her father taught anthropology at the University of Pennsylvania and that her mother worked too, which surprised him. "She's an executive in the fashion industry," Ora Jane explained.

"That explains the sartorial splendor," Shawn chimed in.

"Ooh, impressive," she countered and smiled. "She also taught me to whistle like birds. We have been all over the world listening for birds and the songs they sing."

"Now that's impressive," he countered. "I would love to hear you sing a bird song.

"Well, it's not singing. It's more that I imitate what they whistle, when..."

"I want to hear," he interrupted.

As they sat next to each other on the bench, she put her finger to her lips to shush him.

"Listen," she said.

In the distance Shawn thought he heard a bird singing. Before he could ask if he heard something, Ora Jane repeated the somewhat complicated song Shawn did indeed hear. It was a melody line that swooped down birdlike before rising in an upward pattern that was repeated.

"Wow," said the genuinely excited kid.

"Now close your eyes and listen," she whispered.

She looked over to make sure his eyes were closed before reaching over to give him a quick peck on the lips.

He didn't want to open his eyes, so he let the moment linger. She did also before dropping her bomb.

"Are you Jewish?"

Shawn wasn't sure he wanted to open his eyes.

He tightened up and his mind raced. It was not because of any racism aimed towards him. It was more that he'd been waiting for that day to come when it would happen.

"Why do you ask?" was all he could muster.

"Well, you see my mom is Jewish," she dramatically revealed, eliciting the shocked look she expected from the pronouncement.

"What," he nearly screamed, with his eyes wide open now. "How?"

Over the next few minutes their topic of conversation was racism and Judaism and how the practice of either wasn't part of their households or immediate families.

"That is, except for my uncle Neil," Shawn lamented. "He seems to practice racism all the time and practice being Jewish some of the time. For instance," he continued, "he'll mention not violating the Shabbat if there's something he doesn't want to do. But next Saturday we're driving to Cleveland to see a football game. Let's just say my uncle Neil will not let his religion stand in the way of him having a good time."

Over the past week they practiced in relative privacy at Ora Jane's spacious house where he met Arlene and Liu Whu. They practiced their two Sam Cooke songs and snuck in at least one kiss a day.

Shawn's choice, *Another Saturday Night,* was arranged by them in a bluegrass-country style in honor of a place in Nashville that Ora Jane told him about called the Grand Ole Opry. The two of them traded lines from the melody in the first verse on their respective instruments and then on the very catchy chorus, Ora Jane sang it while simultaneously clapping her hands and stomping her feet.

Playing the violin in a style and manner other than classical music was a totally foreign concept to Shawn. Through the chorus he played the tune as country as only a novice to the style could. He had no idea that the violin was used in country, pop, or any music that wasn't orchestral. When he finally heard Sam Cooke's version of *A Change Is Gonna Come,* it was the first time he'd noticed violins on a pop song.

She explained to him how she learned music; how she learned to write and transcribe from her mother's brother. Unlike Shawn, Ora Jane's uncle was loving, giving, and a human to look up to and learn from. That definitely couldn't describe his sole uncle, Neil.

Now, after all that practice, tomorrow was going to be the day of the talent show. He felt rested even after broken sleep in the car and he wanted to stay in his room and practice some more until his mom came home from visiting a friend to start her weekly Sunday dinner.

Even with his father and uncle in the next room watching the World Series, Shawn was not thinking about baseball. George Knox, Willie Malden, and Lee Morgan were the furthest things from his mind when, like some cosmic messenger, the men in his life brought that day right back into the forefront of his mind.

Neil hadn't intended to spend another day watching sports with his brother-in-law but a friend had given him information about Shawn that he thought they should know. He didn't know Audrey was out with friends. He decided to have a beer and watch a little baseball as she was expected shortly.

Slugger Harmon Killebrew had just hit his first World Series homer in the top of the fourth to make it a 2-1 game in favor of the Dodgers when Neil Bennet and David Berg got their first look at the new car the Chrysler Corporation had in production. In between innings the 1966 Dodge Charger was introduced to America.

"Did you hear that?" David asked excitedly.

"Hear what?" Neil questioned.

"Shh...listen."

"Winston tastes good like a cigarette should..." was the commercial jingle now blaring from the television set.

It was too late.

"That commercial, that car commercial," David said, still way more excited than Neil thought he should be.

"The music on that car commercial," he continued, standing up as he spoke. "I'd know that anywhere. Somebody stole my son's song and they're making money with it."

"What in the hell are you talking about, David," Neil demanded to know.

"That song that Shawn made up. I'm telling you; it was on that car commercial."

"Nonsense," Neil insisted. "Sit down, where in the world would somebody hear anything Shawn made up, or maybe he heard it somewhere. Who knows?"

"Where would Shawn hear something like that?" David asked, calming himself and sitting.

"Actually David, that's something I wanted to talk to you and Audrey about."

"What do you want to talk to Audrey and me about," he snorted, "music on commercials?"

"No," Neil said with a serious tone and looked David in the eye. "No, not that, but where would Shawn hear something like that."

"Now what are you talking about?"

"Look, I was going to wait until Audrey came home to talk to you about this, David, but I found out that Shawn has a nigger girlfriend."

"Again, what are you talking about," David said, outraged by the suggestion. "How do you think Shawn has any girlfriend?"

He paused as he saw the Dodgers' first baseman rounding the bases after hitting a solo homer in the bottom of the fourth to give his team back their two-run cushion at 3-1.

"They certainly don't have...Negroes at that school."

"As much freedom as you two give that boy, you don't know where he met the girl," Neil countered. "For two summers now you let that boy roam Philly with his violin. I'm sure he got a lot more than just music lessons from his nigger girlfriend."

"What are you talking about?" David reiterated.

"Look, I have a friend whose sister goes to the same school who said Shawn's new girlfriend is not one of us, and I don't mean Jewish."

They continued the conversation as Vin Scully wrapped up his announcements at the end of the inning. This time Neil heard it.

It wasn't the announcer saying, "The Chrysler Corporation unveils the future...." It was the music that caught Neil's mouth in motion.

"You're right, David," Neil said, "that's the annoying ditty he used to play on his violin all the time."

The uncle didn't hesitate. He went right to the closed door just off the living room entrance. He barged in as Shawn was working on the part of *Another Saturday Night* where they stomped their feet as they played the chorus.

"Get in here," Neil ordered, in a mean tone.

"What did I do?"

"Just get in here," he repeated.

He walked into the living room with the Dodgers in the middle of a three-run rally on the television.

"Do you know that song that..." his dad started in on him as he walked into the room shadowed by his uncle.

"Umph, Umph," Neil interrupted, repeating the song's rhythm with his grunts and shaking his body while doing it, which made Shawn laugh.

"I don't know that song, Dad," he laughed, "some new dance Uncle Neil learned?"

"Um-umm hmm, hmm, hum-hum-hum-hum," his father sang,

out of tune but hitting those eight notes exactly in the second part of the melody. There was no mistaking it, and Shawn felt like he was turning to the ash that began to reflect in his skin.

It was like his life was flashing before his eyes. The summer of '64, learning the song in different keys, playing it so much that his dad finally asked him what the song title was. He remembered taking a deep breath and calmly lying to his father.

"Oh, it's nothing, Papa," he remembered saying back then. "Just something I made up to warm up."

"It's quite catchy, son," his father had replied.

David Berg hated being lied to.

Why did the song come up now and what did Neil have to do with it? The question sent a wave of fear through Shawn as he relived that summer day he got beat up in a matter of seconds, as his face turned another shade of ash.

"It's something I heard or made up in my head," was the semi-truth that he spieled this time.

"Which is it," Neil said, now menacing and really mad, standing over him. "Did you make it up or did you get it from your nigger girlfriend."

"Papa, what's going on?" Shawn pleaded as his head swirled with questions.

I didn't know Chinese people were called that name, too, and how does Neil know about Ora Jane?

"Neil," David shouted, as he remembered that Shawn had been playing a song by the black singer Sam Cooke.

"Have you no decorum?" David asked, standing up out of his rocker and now thinking how his wife would handle something beyond his control that had gotten toxic quickly. "Don't talk to my son that way."

"You just need to discipline this kid before he gets out of control," an exasperated Neil expressed while sitting in the right rocker across from the television.

"Sit down, Shawn," David said, pointing to the couch to the right of Neil. "I've got an idea. Just sit down, don't say anything and watch the baseball game."

"Papa, I don't want to watch…"

"Sit down, Shawn," he insisted.

Shawn's mind raced, wondering what was going on. When he did try to look at the adults to the left of him, he noticed them glancing at each other and the television. The youngster was so upset at losing this practice time. His mother said she'd be home by 5:30 to start dinner. He'd planned to play his music until dinnertime at 6.

Like yesterday, on their way home from Cleveland, the baseball game started late in L.A. He was not concentrating at all on the baseball game that went to commercials after the bottom of the seventh inning. Instead he noticed the clock on the wall read 5:30.

"Now pay attention," his uncle nearly shouted.

"To what?" Shawn cried and sighed. "There's no baseball on the screen right now."

"Neil, leave the boy alone," he sternly said to his brother-in-law. "Just relax, my son, until your mother comes home."

The ball game moved through the eighth inning quickly, slowed only by the solo home run by Dodgers outfielder Lou Johnson. Two commercial breaks passed by and the Dodge Charger commercial did not air. The frustration that grew between the two men was quite obvious to Shawn.

When Vin Scully announced the lazy pop-up to end the game, Shawn popped up from the couch.

"Game's over, Papa," he pleaded. "I need to practice."

"Sit, Shawn, until your mother comes. She'll be here any minute. You watch the TV."

He moped through another cigarette commercial and another for the new Zenith color television console.

"The Chrysler Corporation unveils the future..." the announcer rang out as the music started.

Shawn was frozen, still hearing that familiar line he learned in the black neighborhood of Philadelphia last summer being played on television. He tensed up.

"The 1966 Dodge Charger is coming..." the TV blared.

Neil smiled.

"Now you told me, son, that you made that song up," his father started in calmly. "Where did you hear it? It's not like the music you played with Mr. Pisterman last year or with that orchestra this year. I noticed you've been playing a different kind of music. Did you hear it at school? Why would you lie to me about something like that?"

Shawn was frozen in fear, remembering the past punishment his dad meted out for the smallest of lies.

"No, David," Neil shot back, in the self-righteous tone he used with his brother-in-law when he knew he was right.

"He didn't hear it at his damn school. He got it from his nigger girlfriend that he started seeing last summer."

Ora Jane! The name screamed in his mind and his hatred of Neil was at an all-time high.

Does that mean I can't be friends with her anymore?

"Son, you're not answering me," his father's voice rose to a higher pitch.

Just then he heard the back kitchen door open. It was his mother.

Shawn turned and ran to meet her with tears beginning to form in his eyes. By the time he reached her, he was in full gulping and sniffing mode. The two male family members followed him to meet her and scream at her at once.

"Momma, momma," Shawn yelled, running into her arms. "Papa's going to whip me."

"Audrey, we've got to start disciplining this boy more before he gets in trouble," was how David Berg greeted his wife with his son's arms wrapped tightly around her.

"I told you, Audrey, you give that boy too much freedom," Neil started, continuing the verbal barrage she was being greeted with. "I told you, you don't know where that boy has been, what he's been doing, or who he's been doing it with on the streets of Philadelphia."

Shawn cried harder which his mother felt as she held him against her breast. That worried her. A momentary thought from the car trip the previous night flew through her mind about how her son used to tell her everything about his life.

He had only told her a couple of days ago about the talent show happening Monday, when she asked about the beautiful song he was playing. When he replied it was a song by a singer named Sam Cooke, she'd wondered how he knew who Cooke was. She didn't remember the conversation at the ball game about him the previous summer.

Audrey Berg was losing the confidence of her only child who was being influenced more by the world. She didn't like the feeling.

"You know, Audrey, I usually don't side with your brother, but he may have a point here," her husband's loquacious assault continued. "And did you know Shawn had a girlfriend."

"A girlfriend?" she replied, trying hard to suppress a smile.

"And do you know how long he's had a girlfriend?" Neil added. "He could be a father for all you know. And she is not one of us."

"Momma," Shawn bawled.

"Whoa, just slow your horses," Audrey screamed, using one of her worn phrases she picked up from the character Hoss from the television show *Bonanza*. "All three of you, quiet."

She pulled Shawn away from her and squatted to his level.

"Honey," she said, kissing a tear falling on his jaw. "I want you to go to your room until I come in there and we'll talk."

Kissing the other cheek, she looked up at her husband and brother.

"Do you know what I'm going to make your father and uncle do?"

"See, there you go Audrey, spoiling that child," her husband railed. "You don't even…"

"David…shh," she ordered, before returning her attention to her son and watching her husband turn to go back to the living room.

"I'm going to make them go buy our favorite meal. You know what our favorite meal is, right?"

"A large sausage and pepperoni pizza, please Mr. Pizza Man," they say simultaneously, with Shawn moping and whispering the words out between gulping back tears.

"Don't you have a talent show tomorrow?" she reminded him.

"Yes," he cried.

"Didn't you have a football game yesterday in Cleveland?"

"Yes, Momma."

"And don't you have the Columbus Day Parade Tuesday?"

"This is sickening," Neil said, before he too left the room.

His mother was trying to make Shawn smile through the tears that he sometimes shed when he was sad over something out of his control, and she was sure this was the case. Her last line worked because Shawn had thought of going to the parade with Ora Jane.

"You've got some practicing to do, don't you?"

"I was trying to tell them that," he replied through the sniffles.

"Go to your room," she sweetly ordered. "I will talk to them and then make them go see Mr. Pizza Man."

Shawn didn't feel like practicing anymore.

He thought how was it possible that the song he picked up from some local musicians in a field in Philadelphia ended up on the World Series broadcast? It was beyond reason and his own worldview as to how such a thing could happen.

Shawn had no idea that the catchy little melody that had gotten him into so much trouble had literally saved a record company called Blue Note Records. They were very close to going out of business when the song, *The Sidewinder,* suddenly began selling in 1964 at a clip ten to twenty times more than any previous release. It sold so fast the company ran out of copies more than once.

He regretted not telling his father that he didn't know the name of the man who made up the song. He had no idea that other people were already stealing from the trumpeter and composer whose name was Lee

180

Morgan. Sean remembers the man saying, "If I get more white folks to sing it, I think I'll have myself a hit."

That must've been what happened, he wondered, *more white folks liked the song.*

What he didn't know was that white people liked it enough for the song to climb all the way to number 25 on the national *Billboard Magazine* sales chart. A white gangster named Morris Levy loved the song so much that he managed to manipulate the copyright and steal money from Morgan for years. Even the Chrysler Corporation embezzled from the composer as they never asked permission to use the song for the World Series. A white person heard it and made it his own.

Shawn fell asleep regretting that Morgan's song must have been stolen. Though he was totally innocent, he felt guilty thinking he was one of those white people.

It felt like hours but it was only 20 minutes before his mother gently woke him up. From that moment, Audrey Berg's son's words flowed out of him from an unrestrained sieve of emotion. He told her everything from the first time he heard the song that he had never heard the title of, up to hearing it less than an hour ago on television.

He was explicit about his misadventure with George Knox. She could fondly hear his admiration for the young black boy who came to his rescue, even if he couldn't remember his name. Somehow he did remember the little boy named Norman whom the kids called Pips and the saxophone player named Joe.

Audrey did remember being vaguely suspicious the day he came home with the sore eye saying he had fallen. As he related how he felt with what and how he was learning about racism, she also remembered the poignant moment leaning down to him at Franklin Field to tell him that people are all the same inside.

Yet she felt immense relief when she realized that the girl Neil's friend's brother said "wasn't one of us" wasn't actually a black girl after all. She later felt guilty that she hadn't felt any guilt in the moment. But in the moment she just wanted to know more about what looked like her son's first love.

Then his mother said two things that helped shaped Shawn's outlook on racism for the rest of his life.

"Honey, you have a good heart," she said, stroking his hair as he leaned against her sitting on his bed. "You'll never lose it, my love. Don't question yourself as to whether you're a racist or not," she continued. "Just remember to treat the Negroes, the Orientals, and the Indians who are not your friends as well as the ones who are."

law—as well as being her initials. Her in-laws accepted the couple since they were kids. She never felt a trace of racism from them, least of all, strangely enough, from Neil.

Over the past fifteen years, like O.J. Simpson, the recently retired football star turned pitchman turned actor, she had managed to succeed in a variety of areas. The stunningly beautiful woman had quite the life adventure before settling down to marry her childhood sweetheart three years prior in 1977. Today she is a rising star attorney at a top law firm that specializes in international immigration laws.

She did her anthropology undergrad degree from Penn where her father taught. She got into law school at Stanford in the Northern California area where he grew up. The thoroughly modern woman saw other men in her six years of schooling but never let Shawn out of her romantic clutches.

Her path also led O.J. to become one of the country's top bird callers. She became well-known within National Audubon Society circles and was awarded lifetime membership into the National Aviary in Pittsburgh. The love of bird songs even led to an act that she and Shawn developed with their respective string instruments and O.J.'s whistling.

Every time she found the time to join him in the endeavor, which they called Birdie & Fly, she was always reminded of the night she said she first fell in love with him. It was that junior high talent show where their version of the Sam Cooke ballad brought tears to the eyes of some teachers. The second Cooke number prompted most everyone in the room to dance to the country atmosphere the party arrangement suggested. The couple won and ended up winning the next two annual talent shows at the school as well.

Music always was and still is something very personal and evocative to the young woman. As good as she was and still is, she could easily pursue music as a professional. However, the thought of making a living off the art was repulsive to her.

Tonight O.J. was very excited for the Philadelphia Phillies only because her husband and the whole city was going crazy. Fifteen years ago, she would have never thought she'd be a sports fan of any kind, but she honestly loves football.

She also loves a winner as she had a brief fling with the 1980 "Miracle on Ice" gold medal-winning American hockey team that stunned the Soviet Union in the Olympics earlier that year. But she didn't watch the Philadelphia Flyers, the city's pro hockey team, when Shawn did. Nor did she really watch the World Series–bound Phillies this year.

Baseball is boring to her, but she absolutely adores sitting with Shawn while he watches. The rhythm of the game allows her to interact with her husband without disturbing his enjoyment. O.J. had always thought of baseball as slow, too meticulous and dull. That is, until the rest of the citizens of the City of Brotherly Love fell in love with this crew that fans dubbed the "Cardiac Kids" because of the incredible number of close games and comebacks they managed to pull off throughout the season.

Tonight was all about Shawn and his favorite sport. She even went to his old neighborhood, to Mr. Pizza Man, to get two large sausage and pepperoni pizzas. O.J. didn't mind that he was late because it gave her a chance to use her new modern kitchen convenience called a microwave oven that was sweeping America.

The oven was used a half-hour later when Shawn finally got home. Thanks to Royals outfielder Amos Otis hitting a two-run homer, his team was down 2-0 at the top of the third inning when he left the building's parking lot. He reached his 15th-floor apartment, kissed his wife, and turned on the television just in time to see Royals outfielder Hal McRae attempt to steal a base with slugging first baseman Willie Aikens up to bat.

"There he goes," said NBC broadcaster Joe Garagiola of the base stealer the instant before Aikens swung. "Well hit, deep to right field, but she's curving foul."

"That was a close one," Shawn said, as he took off his tuxedo jacket.

"It was kind of nippy today, huh, hon?" she asked, wondering if his top was enough for him.

"I was fine, O.J., and the music was great. We played two of Mozart's quartet pieces including the *Spring Quartet*."

"Wow, who decided that?" she asked.

"Holding…" Garagiola, the broadcaster, said of the runner as the very next pitch was being delivered.

"High…deep right-centerfield," the TV continued after Aikens swung. "McBride going back, Maddox going back…home run."

"Wow, today's that guy's 26th birthday," Shawn exclaimed.

"Willie Mays Aiken just broke into his home run track," Garagiola continued.

"How do you know that?" O.J. asked. "You just came in."

"I was listening to the game on the radio in the car."

"Your boys are losing, four-zip," she teased. "Maybe they were just waiting for you to come home to me."

"My boys will be okay."

Shawn was right. In the very next inning, the mood lightened considerably all around town and in the Berg apartment as the Phillies went on a tear. For every slice of pizza Shawn ate, his team scored. With Pete Rose and Mike Schmidt on base, outfielder Bake McBride accented the five-run inning with his first homer of the series.

As Shawn washed his food down with a long swallow of wine, he felt his wife's hand slide up his right thigh. Then she quickly leaned to the left and slipped her tongue into his ear.

"You do know that when they score, you score," she whispered. "That's five times."

He almost did a comedic spit take, he was so surprised by the sudden sensual moves from his wife.

"Do your friends know how silly you are?" Shawn asked.

"Yessss," she purred.

He was just about to kiss her when he heard a melody that seemed to come from the very deep recesses of his psyche. It was a surreal moment as his head swerved towards the sound of the television where his eyes saw a face that he never associated with commercials while his ears were unearthing suppressed childhood memories.

"Listen," he said before she could say anything.

On the television screen was the veteran center of the Los Angeles Lakers basketball team, Kareem Abdul-Jabbar, hawking something called MoneyGram. The music bed behind the NBA great was that very song he'd heard on that Chrysler commercial years ago. It was the ditty he used to warm up his violin playing when he was a kid and the melody that he first heard the day of the first and only violent episode in his life.

"George Knox," he unconsciously blurted out, remembering his nemesis's name immediately before a flood of memories bombarded his memory neurons.

"George Knox," he again said, this time consciously.

"That's not his name," his wife replied, referring to the man she briefly saw before the spot ended. She knew he was an athlete, but could not recall his name.

"You didn't hear the song,"

"What song, honey?"

"I can't believe that just happened," he mumbled. "Uh... I don't know the name of the song."

"Well, who is George Knox?"

"My assassin," Shawn said, laughing.

O.J. had heard part of the story of the mystery song as she was one of the characters in it when they were kids. She also heard bits and pieces as their relationship grew. On this night she heard it all, with all the soaring emotions he experienced at both ballparks—the makeshift one with the black kids and the football stadium with the quartet of racist white men.

The baseball game they were watching suddenly became similar to looking at the Super Bowl, as the commercial breaks were not to be missed. As the players played on the screen, Shawn delivered the most cathartic moments of his life to his best friend ever.

Over the next two innings, he hardly noticed the home team scoring a run in each, making it 7-4, as he bared his soul on memories that he didn't realize would make him so emotional. Between the half innings they waited tensely for the commercial to come back on.

After the top of the seventh inning was over, Shawn took out his violin out and tried to play *The Sidewinder* as fast as he could through every key in the complete circle of fifths. She pleaded mock mercy after the seventh time.

"Sometimes, O.J., I can still feel the pain in my eye after that guy George Knox flattened me," he confessed.

"I wonder if because of that day is the reason I really have no black friends."

"You've been beating yourself up for years, Shawnie," she consoled. "You are not a racist. And what about the opera singers?"

"The opera singers," Shawn laughed. "I've been questioning why the only black friends I've had over the years are opera singers.

"Don't you think that's strange?" he continued.

"Oh, I don't know," she replied.

"Besides, are they my friends, for real," he asked as he glanced at the television in time to see outfielder Garry Maddox fly the first pitch he saw to center field to close out the bottom of the seventh.

The couple was on pins waiting out every commercial, to no avail.

When the game started again, Shawn was paying more attention to the broadcast and was surprised that his team's starting pitcher was rookie Bob Walk. He was the first rookie to start a World Series game in 24 years and, after a rough start, he was still in the game.

"George Brett," Garagiola growled from the television about the player who had a historic season with his batting average. "He just captures all of America as he chases .400."

"Oh, I can feel the Cardiac Kids are about to get into their routine," Shawn said to his wife, who was quite concerned for her husband's emotional state of mind.

As if on cue, Brett hit a ball to the wall for a double.

"There's Tug McGraw in the Phillies' bullpen," said the Cincinnati Reds All-Star pitcher Tom Seaver, who was working the game as an analyst for NBC. "And I know manager Dallas Green don't want to see that unless it wins the ball game for them."

As the other analyst, Tony Kubek, wondered whether Walk's rookie status was a factor, the Phillies' pitching coach, Herm Starrette, bounded out of the dugout and headed to the pitcher's mound.

"They're getting ready to go to a commercial now and I bet that song is going to come on this time."

Instead, Starrette left the rookie in and Garagiola let the local stations do a quick identification.

"So George Brett is on at second base. It's a 7-4 ball game," the announcer restarted. "Philadelphia's out in front. Willie Mays Aikens is the batter."

"Hey, ain't that the guy celebrating a birthday today?" O.J. asked.

"Yep, and he's juiced."

On the second pitch of the at-bat, the pitch got away from the catcher Bob Boone and the runner, Brett, moved to third.

"I guess your Cardiac Kids are living up to their name," she said, on edge.

"Yep, and he's juiced," Shawn repeated.

The words were barely out of his mouth when Aikens once again hit a two-run homer.

"If he's not tired, he's gonna be tired after that shot," Garagiola said of the rookie. "Willie Mays Aikens really into his home run trot now. It's a 7 to 6 ball game."

"There's Dallas Green going out to the mound," Seaver said. "Bob Walk, I think, has had enough.

"Good shot of Willie Mays Aikens in the dugout," he finished.

"And we're going to have a break in the action as Bob Walk gets a good hand," Garagiola broadcast. "We'll be right back after these messages from your local station."

"I'm Kareem Abdul-Jabbar introducing MoneyGram," were the next words out of the screen.

"There it is...shh..." O.J. said.

"Oh honey, that's amazing," an exuberant Shawn screamed when it was over.

"And you don't know that name of the song."

"No, no. I remember George Knox, the pain in my eye, and that the sax player's name was Joe.

"I think there was a little kid there too named Norman. I just wish

I could remember the name of the guy who saved my life that day."

"At least we will find the song and maybe the name of the trumpet player too," O.J. says assuredly.

Thursday, October 16, 1980
In true Cardiac Kids fashion, the Phillies held on to win Game 1 when reliever McGraw did come out of the bullpen and stopped the Royals rally, eking out the win 7-6. It was the first Phillies World Series win since 1915.

They won Game 2 in heart-stopping fashion as well. Down two runs 4-2 in the bottom of the 8th, they staged a four-run rally highlighted by a two-run double by future Hall of Fame third baseman Mike Schmidt.

The city of Philadelphia was feeling pretty good on the afternoon that O.J. went on the mission to solve the mystery from her husband's childhood. After a couple of telephone conference calls, an office meeting, and securing her tickets and final plans to meet an international client in Sri Lanka, she set off on her plan.

After some easy inquiries she found herself at 10 Third Street in downtown Philadelphia not far from her office. That address was the home of the legendary Philly record store, 3rd Street Jazz & Rock.

The narrow dank entrance led to a long shotgun room that was filled with several long rows of bins of albums and music she found strange but pleasurable. When O.J. looked up the back wall of the place, some 20 feet back, there was a fascinating montage that hypnotized her.

"What can I do for you, Miss?" A scruffy short man with a scraggly salt-and-pepper beard and loud voice startled her.

"Oh, I..." she stammered, looking around for more pleasant help, with her eyes again stopping on the back wall.

"I'm just looking," she decided to say with her eyes towards the art at the back of the room that was like a magnet to her.

The store had maybe thirty patrons of various ages and races. As she walked to the back, she glanced down a flight of stairs under a huge sign that read "Rock." She went right to the cashier who was waiting on two youngsters whom the clerk knew by name, a black kid named Chris and a stout young white kid named Joey. *They couldn't be quite teenagers,* she thought, remembering the stories her husband revealed about his youth.

"Hey Joey, tell Papa John I will be at his gig tonight."

"I will, Van," the kid said, clinging to whatever new piece of vinyl he was carrying.

"Can I help you find something, Miss?" the clerk asked.

"Yes, I'm looking for a song I heard on a commercial last night during the ball game," she inquired, hoping the song was popular enough that the clerk would know it instantly.

"Well, just because it was on a commercial doesn't mean it's something on record."

"I've got a feeling it is a well-known song because my husband heard it on another commercial when he was a kid."

"Hmmm... are you sure it's a jazz tune?" the clerk inquired suspiciously.

"My husband thinks he heard a jazz band play it before," she snapped, not appreciating being doubted.

"Can you hum it?" asked the thin tall white man to O.J., who assessed that with his long, white-tinged, thin hair, he was in his mid-40s.

She hit the third note of the song.

"Oh, that's *The Sidewinder* by Lee Morgan."

"I told you it was popular," she crowed excitedly, pulling a pad and paper from her purse. "Now, what's the name of it?"

"The song is titled *The Sidewinder*, just as it sounds, all one word. It's by a Philly guy, Lee Morgan."

"And what's your name, sir?"

"Van, ma'am," he politely replied. "You say it was on a commercial on the ball game last night?"

"Yes," she said before pausing and putting the pad away. "Now Van, this may be a strange question, but is it at all possible that there is a sax player in Mr. Morgan's band named Joe?"

"That would be Joe Henderson," he said, surprising her with his quick response. "Why do you ask?"

"It's a long story. Do you have it available?"

Van looked at his growing line at the register and realized he didn't have the time or patience to listen to the story.

"I'll get someone to help you out," he said, motioning to the next customer in line.

"Hey, Bill," he projected a few aisles over, before looking back at her. "Bill, our manager, he'll get you right what you need.

"She needs a copy of *The Sidewinder*." He raised his voice back to Bill, "Says she heard it on the ball game last night."

"I heard it too," Bill responded, pointing to O.J. to meet him down and over a few racks of albums.

"I could be wrong," he commented flirtatiously, as the beautiful stylish Asian woman walked towards him, "but you don't look like a real big jazz fan."

She was dressed in a seasonal orange and brown mini-skirt that she bought less for the season than because they matched the colors of the Cleveland Browns.

"How could you tell?" she asked sarcastically as he approached the rack of albums marked 'Miscellaneous M.'

"I get paid to know these things," he responded, perusing the albums until he got to a divider with the words 'Lee Morgan,' written in giant Magic Marker ink.

"I think you should get *The Best of Lee Morgan* so you can hear his other hits."

"He had other hits?" she excitedly asked.

"Maybe one more that they definitely played on the radio."

"Van over there said Morgan's from Philly. Is he still here? Can I go see him?" she pleaded, getting more excited with each word.

"No no, he died a few years ago."

"Oh, shit," was her honest reaction.

"He was murdered, while he was performing on stage too."

"My goodness," she blurted out as she tried to stifle the tears that suddenly began filling her tear ducts.

"I'm so sorry," the store manager said, reaching out to put his hands on her shoulder. "I didn't mean for that to come out like that."

O.J. took a few seconds to calm herself.

"I'm okay...It's...It's just you have no idea how much that song means to my husband," she explained, now losing the battle to fight back some tears.

"Are you from Philadelphia," she continued as he nodded yes.

"Well, do you remember the riots a few years ago when we were young?"

"August of '64," he replied quickly.

"You won't believe this but a week after the riots, my husband found himself, a dorky white Jewish kid, beat up in a black neighborhood."

"That happened a lot back in those days," Bill responded.

"Well, he thinks the man who wrote that song may have saved his life."

"That's some story," he laughed nervously. "The song saved his life. How so?"

"Not the song," she says. "The man who wrote the song."

The man suddenly puts both of his palms to his face.

"I'm getting a wild feeling, but this can't be happening."

"Well it is and it did," O.J. snapped as if he didn't believe her.

"No...I mean..." he stalled, thinking. "Did your husband play violin?"

"Still does," she says defiantly, as if under hostile questioning instead of taking in the context of what he is asking.

"Shawn Berg..." he whispered, at first unassured and then wistfully.

"Nooooo...." she said, once she realized what he'd said.

"Shawn Berg is your husband," Bill almost screamed, getting excited.

"Nooooo," O.J. repeated.

"Yes, yes, yes," he exclaimed, getting more excited.

The tears flowed more as her arms reached out to request a hug.

They rocked and in the middle of the embrace, she whispered.

"So do you know George Knox?"

Bill, or Willie Malden as he was known as a boy, broke the hug and laughed.

"Does his eye still hurt?" he asks, laughing more.

Tuesday, October 21, 1980

When Shawn opened the envelope he got from the messenger on Monday, he knew exactly who had sent it. It was a bleachers ticket to Game 6 of the World Series attached to a note that read, "Here's an invitation to see someone you haven't seen in a long time."

There's no sense in calling her, because she'd never admit it, he thought.

"This has Campy written all over it," he voiced.

"Campy" was the name Shawn adopted for the very bold, very flirtatious alter ego that periodically O.J. pulled out in often flamboyant ways, in very public places, in towns and venues where they weren't known. She played a lot of sensual games and always had surprising pleasurable sexual activities planned while they were dating. The less time they had together as life, work, and marriage intervened, the more elaborate her romantic schemes became.

He gave her the name Campy five years ago when O.J.'s work took her to a very important worldwide conference on immigration in Paris and he couldn't join her right away. So he flew alone on a later flight. She arrived to the airport and met him at the gate dressed as a very expensive call girl. When the woman with the long white feathered boa, star-spangled blue and white halter top, neon blue hot pants, fishnet stockings, and clear platform heels walked up to him and locked arms, he almost fainted.

"It's okay, Fly Boy," she rasped, in a loud, overdone Brooklyn accent while smacking the gum in her mouth. "Your wife could never pick you up like I can."

When he realized it was O.J., the embarrassment he felt from every eye at the gate that was looking at them was overwhelmed by the laughter that erupted from deep inside him.

"Fuck these people; they'll never see us again," she flaunted, looking at the inquisitive eyes as they laughed their way through the terminal.

When the Paris police approached the pair while waiting at baggage claim, O.J. launched into another persona. She flipped from being a New York prostitute to a high-class Parisian hooker and in perfect French told the two cops off as she reached into her purse for a very official-looking badge. They backed down quickly.

"Wow, that wasn't your passport you showed them," Shawn said, between guffaws. "What did you say to them?"

"I told them to fuck off," she said, right back into the loud Brooklyn whore tone. "I showed them I was a guest of their government and that you were my husband, to leave me the fuck alone and let me play with my man."

Shawn bowled over with laughter as she flung the feathered garment back around her neck and put her hands on her hip, shook her backside, and sighed loudly.

"Shit, they should know better than to mess with a hard-working girl."

He dubbed her character "Campy" at that moment.

What on earth can she have planned in the bleachers at Veterans Stadium, he pondered, as his imagination wandered.

O.J. never told Shawn that she had found the title of that elusive song, the trumpet player Lee Morgan, and the boy who saved his life. Her only regret was that she wouldn't see the fruits of her altruistic ruse.

After the messenger dropped off the envelope at 3rd Street Jazz & Rock on Monday, Bill, too, thought of a woman. But his initial feeling and reaction, of dread and chills, were totally opposite from Shawn's when he saw the bleacher ticket.

He stared at the invitation.

"Here's an invitation to see someone you haven't seen a long time."

"A long time is relative," he mumbled.

All of his celebrity music friends, his rich associates in the financial world, and close buddies knew that Bill and his brother Bobby owned luxury season box seats at venues for Philly's professional football, basketball, and baseball teams. He was very excited about Game 6 tonight. He knew he wouldn't be sitting with the person he suspected sent the ticket. He never thought of O.J.

"Hey Van," Bill said to his co-worker who was restocking records that had gathered at the cashier's table. "Wanna go to the ball game tonight? It's going to be quite the party if they win."

Ever since O.J. left the store, he assumed they were coming back that week. So Bill was back to whiplashing his head towards the door every time a customer entered. Every white guy his age who walked in, he immediately thought it could be Shawn Berg. It wasn't that long ago when he was snapping his head towards the front door hoping it wasn't Erica Thomas.

"Whoa," Van lit up seeing the ticket while holding an album to file in his hand, "Where the hell'd you score this?"

Bill handed Van the invitation that accompanied the ticket.

"Oh," Van replied, handing the paper back then filing away the latest Barry White album *The Message Is Love.*

"Let me see that," Bill asked of the White album.

"You know that's the first album on his own label, right," Van said, handing it over.

"Yeah and it's with CBS, which you know makes me feel close to it."

"That woman just won't stop, will she?" Van spoke back to the invitation. "Just will not give up that thing of yours.

"You know ever since she told that cop all she wants to do is suck you," he continued laughing, "she gives all of us white boys a complex every time she walks in here."

"She ain't supposed to be walking up in here," Bill responded disgustingly.

"I haven't seen her in weeks."

"Yeah, I know. I thought I was done looking. But I'm new to this. How do you know when someone has stopped stalking you."

"I quit looking for her, too," Van said, taking the ticket out of his hand. "But she's a beautiful woman. I think I can suffer though Game 6 of the World Series with her."

Ever since Shawn left his old neighborhood ice cream shop back in 1964, Willie, now Bill, had wondered how his life compared to his own as they grew. By his own estimation he doesn't think a week or ten days have passed since that day 16 years ago where he didn't use his idea of Shawn's fate as inspiration to strive to make sure his own lot was on par, especially when it came to money and success in music.

He never thought of or compared his personal life to what he thought Shawn's had become. That is, until he met O.J. Then, in retrospect, he knew he'd lost in that part of life's race to bliss. While he'd had something of a charmed life professionally, his love life was one long disaster after another. He called himself "a victim of long-term relationships."

He'd never met or fallen as fast for a woman like Erica Thomas. It was a relatively short relationship of eight months. For him the downward spiral began one day in the store when she turned into a violent jealous monster. A very young mini-skirted customer had been a little flirtatious with Bill and when she walked away, Erica approached him with her nostrils flaming.

"You're fucking her, aren't you," she said loud enough in the back of the store for the owner to hear at the front.

He tried to break up with her for ten months, eventually ending up in court to get an order of protection. When served with the paper by a sheriff at her home, she took her brand of hysterical love/hate passion towards Bill to a whole different sneaky and unpredictable level for another ten months. No one in the store doubted the source of the ticket.

Six weeks ago was the last time they had seen her, when she paid the UPS driver a hundred dollars to let her walk a package in. With the driver's manifest in her hands, she headed straight for Bill, who thought she had a weapon.

"That was right after Jerry said he thought she could kill you," Van recounted, still holding the ticket while admiring two scantily clad punk-rockers heading downstairs to their district of vinyl in the store.

"And now that she knows cops won't do anything even though I have an order of protection, there's no telling what crazy thing she might do."

"At that game," Van said ominously, "she would have you out in the open...she could say or do anything to you, even shoot you. They don't search people going into stadiums, especially women. And if they do, they're looking for bottles."

"Cops, man," Bill picked up the beat, "they let women get away with shit.

"Did I ever tell you 'bout the time my mom slapped a pig?"

Officer O'Malley never did get his chance to exact revenge on the Malden boys, as he was brought up on corruption charges not long after the welts healed from Mrs. Malden's slap. Unlike many in his neighborhood, Bill escaped interacting with police except for a memorable time after college and in the case of Erica Thomas.

3rd Street, as it was known in Philly, had three encounters with Ms. Thomas that required the services of the Philadelphia Police Department. Bill's order of protection was a joke each time. Instead of the legal deterrent it was meant to be, to keep Erica away from him, it became a way to insult his manhood, among other things.

The level of vulgarity varied as much as the race of the law enforcement officer working on their stand-up comedy. From the Puerto Rican and black pair of peace officers who just didn't think his small piece was worth their effort, to the Italian and Mexican who suggested all he needed to do was abuse her.

He had always been reluctant to call the police on her because of the horrid things he'd heard through his sister that Philly police subject black woman to. Then the attacks grew so weird and she was so relentless at one time that even Cassandra, who grew to be a lawyer representing children of incarcerated parents, agreed Erica was a little too weird and a bit too aggressive.

Baseball was his weakness but even as much as he attended, she never knew his season tickets guaranteed him post-season seats. He couldn't imagine what her game was for Game 6 of the 1980 World Series; he just knew he'd be sitting with his brother and she'd be sitting with Van.

"How much you want for the ticket," Van asked the day of the game.

"Enjoy the ball game, my friend," Bill said, assuring Van the ticket was his free and clear.

"I will thank her for it," He laughed.

Just then the creaky front door opened and once again Bill's thoughts turned to the last time the Philadelphia Phillies were this close to a championship when he met Shawn Berg.

He had reasons to be emotional when O.J. revealed who her husband was. Unlike his childhood counterpart, Bill never forgot Shawn's name. In fact, since the day the mysterious Asian lady showed up, he came to realize that part of his goal in life was to best Shawn.

When he first saw the scrawny white boy behind the tree a decade and a half ago, he reasoned right away that wasn't the white kid in his alternate universe. However, since that day in the ice cream shop splurging on Lee Morgan's money, now he's come to realize that Shawn was indeed one of his main motivations besides his parents, brother, and sister.

Mr. and Mrs. Malden achieved the dream of every parent regardless of race and that is to have all your kids achieve major success. Robert Malden Sr. wanted to live his professional aspiration through his children. The chance to study law had eluded the elder Malden mostly because of the mores of the nation's Jim Crow laws. He was determined to live vicariously through his children, despite their own wishes.

The kids' old man felt he hit the jackpot when the older two explored two totally opposite ends of jurisprudence. The greedy parent was disappointed when his youngest at first drifted totally the other way.

"It's your fault," Bill said, in a teenage shouting match with his father upon declaring music his major in college. "You were the one who brought a piano into the house."

The elder Malden has always been eternally grateful that besides the Philly baseball team and the myriad of r&b vocal groups in the city, only his oldest son and daughter held more sway over Bill coming up. When his brother insisted that Bill attend a lecture with him by a radical Harvard law professor named Derrick Bell before declaring a major, he had no idea it would profoundly change his life.

Eventually Bill came up with the humorous line, for the few nerds that got the joke, that the four pillars of his success are held by four teams: Malcolm X and Dr. King; Kenny Gamble and Leon Huff; Bobby and Cassandra Malden; and the Bell Brothers—Thom and Derrick Bell. If they didn't get the joke that the relatively unknown man named Bell couldn't compare to the Philadelphia legend named Thom, Bill was happy to tell them who Derrick was, including his father.

"Dad, you're just going to be so happy," he remembered years ago working on getting an approving smile on his father's face.

"A lawyer convinced him to change my major. And Dad," he said back then, with way too much enthusiasm, "and it was this Harvard law professor, Derrick Bell, who made me want to change my major to...."

He hung on for dramatic effect and to take the growing smile on his father's face to its furthest reaches before it drooped when he revealed his choice.

"...Economics."

All of those aforementioned people may have been his main influences growing up but Shawn was there too, even though he wasn't.

Like Shawn, race played a part of important decisions in Bill's development. And like Shawn and hundreds of thousands of other kids of their generation, the seismic events of 1964 and 1965 shaped their views of others who did not look like themselves.

These two kids from different sides of the same town had different environments and cultures. Certain events, though, kept their alternative Philly universes in tandem. Less than 90 days after they met in 1964, the shooting death of Sam Cooke became part of their shared legacy. Less than 90 days after that, the Malden family dynamic took a seismic shift with another violent gun death, that of Malcolm X.

Unlike Shawn, and unlike his early depictions of his fictitious white cross-town equivalent, Bill had siblings. That makes a huge difference in those very impressionable early years of life and those precious preteen years.

Those two iconic gun deaths galvanized and forever changed the trajectory of Bobby Malden's relationship with white people and Bill's view of both his older brother and sister.

Cooke's murder just stunned the music world in general and a large percentage of progressive young black people in particular. For those burgeoning post–civil rights/pre–black revolutionary youngsters, he meant more than just a pop singer who crossed over to white tastes. Percolating under the fiery rhetoric of the new, very visible vocal leaders were a class of forerunners, both liberal and conservative, who were lawyers, scholars, and economists contemplating a future black economy.

The famous meeting with Cooke, Malcolm X, Ali, and Jim Brown to an extent championed these lesser known but vitally important heroes. At least that's the way Bobby and Cassandra Malden took it. Law and statistics became as much a part of the black civil rights philosophy they shared with their little brother as music and sports. The more the first two notions dominated the older siblings' lives, the more somehow Bill managed to combine all four.

All the violent assassinations of black leaders had the effect of metamorphosing the Malden family. To Bill it was Malcolm's death in 1965 that took the oldest Malden kid down some unforeseen twisted and warped legal paths. Then three years later when Dr. King died the same way, Cassandra was jolted towards her future down her more righteous legal lanes.

Bobby immediately became a conspiracy theorist when Malcolm, too, died at the hands of someone black with a gun. He worried that there were now black hit men out there to kill Brown and Ali. He predicted both athletes would be forced to quit or be murdered within a couple of years if they kept encouraging a black economy.

When Brown was indeed pressured to quit the very next year, Bobby crowed, calling the Cleveland Browns owner, Art Modell, racist. The row between the player and owner was over Brown's participation in the making of the movie *The Dirty Dozen*, which was behind schedule, causing the player to miss training camp. After he began incurring huge daily fines, he quit, even though he was reigning MVP and unquestionably the best professional football player alive.

After digging into just how much the highest paid player in football was giving up, and finding out that he once threatened to quit unless teammates, including Walter Beach, got a raise, Brown became more of a personal hero to Bill. A dig into his incredible record-breaking statistics contributed to the younger Malden's growing obsession with numbers.

A year later in 1967 when Ali was also forced out of his ability to earn his substantial living, both of the Malden brothers were affected. Bobby once again crowed loudly as a worthy soothsayer, but Bill thought with a hard edge this time. It was his own conspiracy theory about his brother that began when it became important for him to point how black people were responsible for his heroes' deaths.

While home for a weekend from his Ivy League college one weekend, the pre-law student planted ideas in his high school-age brother. It was a twisted diatribe about how black folks' lack of unity led to Ali's refusal to be inducted into the U.S. Army, and thus him being stripped of his right to box. Bill regarded that weekend as the start of his brother's long slide into conservatism. It also affirmed that after Malcolm's death his brother began to develop a form of black self-hatred.

The horrifying affliction was hastened as Bobby flew through law school and almost immediately after passing the bar literally bumped into a large, seven-figure accident settlement. On the strength of that one case, he quickly scored a smaller, multi-million-dollar payment. Both of his clients were white.

As the first lawyer in the Malden clan, Bobby chose to chase ambulances. He made his father extremely proud as he became very good at it. Eventually he assembled an elite team of legal eagles who followed siren lights to hospitals and accidents or crime scenes.

The more success he had, the whiter he became. He became what Bill termed a racial shapeshifter. Whenever they were around any family members, he saw the normal Bobby he grew to love and idolize as a kid. He developed different archetypes for everybody else.

He had accents for different types of black people. In their old neighborhood he had more of a 'hood ghetto sound with the number of consonants dropping in and out depending on the property value he was standing on. The side of Market Street he was on, and the race and gender he was addressing, determined how much hip black lingo he let loose through his prattle.

The more Bobby headed downtown towards Market Street, the more Caucasian nuances came to the fore in his speech. The closer he got to City Hall, the more his persona changed. At ground zero of his whiteness, in a courtroom in front of a judge, he sounded like a corn-fed Nebraskan instead of a black man from Philadelphia.

Inside, what really frightened and outraged Bill was that when

in love with the '64 team and so many also-rans. Now they were on the cusp of greatness and he thought of his childhood chums and how back then only Norman, the little kid they called "Pips," and the white boy Shawn Berg were the only ones he knew who were the true Phillies fans when they almost won it with Richie Allen and Johnny Callison.

Norman was becoming a successful jazz musician, someone told him, but he hadn't heard from him in close to ten years. These were his thoughts as he gave the waiter his credit card. By the time the waiter returned, he was lamenting the fact that Shawn hadn't come to the store like O.J. said he would.

It's a shame I didn't get a phone number from her, he thought, as he rose from the café to catch a cab to the ballpark.

The City of Brotherly Love was high with anticipation that Bill could feel as he instructed the driver to take the slow, expensive way. He was truly looking forward to telling every white man in the luxury boxes that Bobby tried to impress how he hated the Phillies when they were kids.

It was an ironic twist considering the reason Bobby hated the early 60s Phillies was for their lack of respect for black players. He also thought maybe that was a good way to start the discussion on his brother's weird shapeshifter quirk.

Shawn, on the other hand, was truly looking forward to his quirky seatmate when he arrived to the park. After making his way to the bleachers he was extremely disappointed to find the seat next to him empty. He kept looking around for O.J. in whatever guise she and Campy had planned for him. But once the big television monitors began showing pitcher Steve Carlton warming up in the bullpen, it began to sink in exactly where he was in life.

Lefty, as Carlton was adoringly called, had not only replaced Jim Bunning as his all-time favorite Phillies pitcher, but also indeed had overtaken Callison as his all-time favorite Philadelphia baseball player. Shawn never thought he'd ever like a pitcher as much as he did Carlton.

"Let's go get 'em, Lefty," Shawn screamed out, as much on instinct more than the reality that Carlton was going to hear him from the back of the bleachers.

He was such an amazing player that he even had fans from other teams who admired him, as long as he wasn't pitching against them. The hard-core Phillies fans liked Shawn and Bill who stayed with the team when they were doormats of the league in the early 70s and adored Carlton. This was his ninth season with the team for which he had already won two Cy Young Awards for being recognized as the best pitcher in his league, including 1972. That was his first year with the team for which he won an astounding 27 games for a team that won only 59 the whole season.

"That was almost 50 percent of the total for the whole team that year," came a shout from an older, gray-haired woman dressed in a resplendent white with red pinstripes Number 20 Mike Schmidt jersey.

The woman was seated in the row in front and to the right of Shawn. She made him think of his mom, who these days would hardly be the only knowledgeable woman at any sporting event.

Speaking of women at sporting events, where's O.J? he thought, looking around the gorgeous, gussied-up park. He knew she wasn't on the field, but to soak it in he stared at the special World Series bunting on the field where the starting lineups were about to be introduced.

"I hear that Jim Bunning just won a local state senate seat in Kentucky," said a gray-bearded man with a big smile down a few rows and to the left of Shawn, who seemed to be the exact contrast of the evil racist old man from the Eagles football game at Franklin Field when he was a kid.

"Can you imagine that, Bunning, a state senator?" said the man to Shawn's immediate right who was chaperoning a quartet of four teenage boys with another man five seats down.

"No, I can't," Shawn replied, before introducing himself to Tom, the 30-something father of two of the boys and uncle to the others with his brother Matt at the other end. "He's just trying to find himself. I can't imagine Jim Bunning being successful in politics."

As the introduction of first the Royals started and eventually continued on with the introduction of the home team, fans around Shawn began to question him about the empty seat next to him. It first began as a guessing game with the four college men to the left of the empty seat. Then a heightened mystery started to unfold after Shawn regaled all around about the high jinks and games O.J. had played with him in Philly and around the world.

"One time she had me meet her at Independence Park where she and two of her opera singer friends in full British Redcoat costumes prepared a little musical about our private life."

"Wow, that's pretty intense," said one of two men sitting directly behind Shawn dressed in Number 32 Phillies home jerseys. His jersey said "Phil" and the other said "Lee."

"Is she a good-looking woman?" asked the man labeled Lee, who, when Shawn looked back, realized they were twins.

"Another time she had to work in Scotland," Shawn continued on, ignoring the question, "and she showed up in kilts with a bagpipe player at a hotel playing silly love songs."

"Now I've got to ask," the coed next to the empty seat managed between beer burps, "is she good-looking?"

Shawn egged them on with the couple's most recent escapade in Paris.

"I don't find that funny," the older lady to the front right exclaimed. "That all sounds like she's trying to embarrass you."

"It's her way of showing love, Miss," Shawn said, laughing.

"Sounds like a way to keep a marriage exciting," Tom, to Shawn's right, said, and laughed nervously.

Then he brought his voice down to a whisper into Shawn's ear.

"I could use some excitement with my wife," he complained.

Most of that was forgotten by all except Shawn once the game started and Carlton started mowing down the Royals in the first three innings. Then the earth shook at the Vet in the bottom of the third, when first Pete Rose, who was nicknamed "Charlie Hustle," beat out a perfect bunt single to load the bases after a walk and error.

The crowd simmered when Kansas City's manager Jim Frey came out and brought the action to a halt by taking starter Rich Gale out. Shawn daydreamed about O.J. during most of the pitching change. Putting in reliever Rennie Martin didn't matter since the next batter, Schmidt, got the house party rocking when he singled, giving the Phillies a 2-0 lead.

Van was in no hurry to pull the fast one on Erica so he entered the park on the opposite side of the massive bleachers section at "The Vet," as locals called Veterans Stadium. He entered the gates on the home plate side of the massive edifice that was now also home to the Eagles NFL football team.

Walking up to the 700 level, Van looked down at the field towards home plate, then to the far reaches of right field and up to the bleachers area from where he'd be watching the game. As he began his long walk, he marveled at the electricity in the park where everyone was aware Philadelphia could be winning a championship on this night. He was hoping that by the time he got to the seat, Erica would've realized that the jig was up and would have sulked away.

"I just hope for your sake that she told the hit man she paid to kill me that I was a black man," Bill had teased him at the store earlier that day, when the theory returned to the notion that she wanted her former lover dead. Van was under strict instructions not to divulge any information to anyone about Bill or how he got the ticket.

He ended up watching the exciting, two-run third inning in the back of the bleachers in the standing-room-only area. Van peeked down into the upper bleachers and saw a nondescript white man next to the empty seat. He didn't look like a hit man.

The guy in question seemed to have a familiarity with all those around. That led Van to believe that whatever Erica had planned had blown up and squatters from the standing areas had copped a seat. With all the jumping up and down after Mike Schmidt knocked in two runs, Van now wanted to sit.

Arriving at the assigned row, he navigated the couple at the end of the row. The college guys did the math right away and realized there was only one seat for the newcomer.

"Hey Shawn, your wife has arrived," the first one to get up declared.

The heads of the Phil-Lee twins swerved left immediately.

"That's a hell of a costume," bellowed one of the costumed brothers.

"And I was expecting fishnet stockings," roared the other.

"Who are you and where is O.J.," a confused Shawn demanded to know, looking up from his seat.

"Who the fuck are you," an even more incredulous Van reacted, "and how in the hell do I know where O.J. Simpson is?"

"You didn't tell me you were gay," Tom, the dad to the right, whispered to Shawn. "I could use some help with my nephew."

"You were so right; she is stunning," said the coed next to Van.

"What are you guys all talking about?" Van asked, as he stood looking down at those looking at him instead of the field at U.L. Washington, the first Kansas City batter in the top of the fourth inning.

"What's going on here, sir, is I was expecting my wife to join me here," Shawn explained.

"Well, unless you're married to a man," came a heretofore unknown voice from two rows back, "you're still expecting your wife."

"What makes you think your wife had this ticket?" a very confused Van asked, holding the ticket in his hand and checking the seat number. "Actually I was expecting a woman to be here with me."

"Ooh, the plot thickens," the old lady pretending not to be listening chimed in.

"Who were you expecting?" Shawn inquired, with a whiff of indignation.

"Not you," Van said, maybe a little too tersely as he sat down to watch Carlton continue to mow the Royals down.

There were a few moments of silence between the two as the others drove their attention in and out of the situation between the

"That's how all this started," Shawn said, looking around. "What happened to Lee Morgan?"

"He was murdered in New York back in '72, at a club ironically called Slugs'."

"Noooo. Nooo."

"When I told your wife I think I almost made her cry," he confessed. "I was thrilled when she told me that you kept playing your violin."

He then asked about O.J. and the two of them dug and inquired, changing subjects at a fast pace. They were trying to fill in the blanks of suppositions and false realities of race, romance, and what they thought about each other growing up. On the subject of the long relationship Shawn had with his wife and their vast, long, and expansive romance, Bill was quite envious. He wondered if he would ever know what it would be like to be a one-woman man for the rest of his life.

"We actually bonded in sixth grade over Sam Cooke, believe it or not," Shawn crowed. The point was made that music was important in both of their lives.

"Wow, we have some of the same heroes," Bill suggested, just as the Phillies were coming to bat in the bottom of the eighth inning. "You may not believe this but Sam Cooke was a big reason I got into economics."

"Oh, I believe it," Shawn emphasized, realizing it would be a surprise. "That meeting he had with Malcolm X almost got my family and me into a fight. Well, actually, it did."

"What could you be talking about?" Bill incredulously asked. "I didn't even know white folks knew or cared about shit like that."

Shawn let out a big laugh.

"Actually, that kind of shit scares a lot of insecure white people," he told Bill, before expounding on his experience with the racist men at the Eagles game during the Phillies' historic 1964 collapse.

Bill was just entranced by the story and by the novelty of hearing of such stupid racism from a white man. As the two of them went back and forth back between the nastiness of that day, they would momentarily get back to the excitement of the '64 team of their childhood. Meanwhile, the Phillies at the dawn of the 80s were just coming up to bat in the eighth inning, still leading 4-1.

The frenzy was building outside the clubhouse before maybe the home team's last at-bat for the years. It didn't matter; inside two fans were still reliving the championship the Phillies lost sixteen years earlier. When the subject turned to the Cleveland Browns, Bill perked up

212

even more.

"You mean you were at a Cleveland game, watching Jim Brown play that weekend when the Phillies were falling out of first place?" Bill asked, as Shawn nodded to the affirmative.

"I love Jim Brown. Just think had he not quit when he did."

"I'm telling you, dude, it's amazing," Bill exclaimed. "We have some of the same heroes."

"We went to a game at Franklin Field the year they won in '64 and we went the next year in Cleveland. It was their home game where they received their championship rings.

"My mom was something," Shawn continued. "She was way ahead of her time when it came to women really knowing about sports. In that game with the Eagles she was spewing out stats and facts about the Browns that had those Eagles fans' heads spinning.

"I could tell they didn't like her and not just because the Browns were kicking the Eagles' ass," he continued, getting more loquacious with each sip of beer. "But it was bittersweet for me with our boys losing."

They were really concentrating and into the memories while also being aware of the potentially historic memory in front of them on the television screen. Each of them kept glancing at the monitor, but the fact that the Phillies had just gone down meekly, three-up-three-down, in the bottom of the eighth of Game 6 of the World Series, was almost an afterthought.

"I'll never forget that whole week," Bill nodded. "I remember trying to stop myself from crying, repeating over and over, 'It's just a game, it's just a game.'

"That was the day your hero, Johnny Callison, hit three homers, right?" Bill continued. "Man, I prayed hard for Richie Allen to come through in that game."

"I would have been crying too except Jim Brown was running all over the Eagles," Shawn recalled, almost spilling his drink.

"But what was really made an impression on my life that day was my mom. You see, my racist uncle drove me to that game because my parents had something to do and met us there.

"As we drove to the game, my uncle went on this tirade about how Jim Brown used his clout to help his teammates get a raise. He was a die-hard Browns fan, like my mom and dad, they're all from Cleveland. But on this day he was pissed at a player named Walter Beach."

"Whoa," said Bill, clinching his fist about to explode, wanting to break into the conversation. "This is so amazing. Go on."

"So just to piss my uncle off," Shawn went on, "when we had this little agitation with those racist guys, I started talking about how good this Walter Beach guy was. I really didn't know who he was. I just wanted to get under the skin of my uncle.

"But then, Willie, I'm telling you, something cosmic happened. It was like I started communicating with Walter Beach. I still remember his number: 49.

"Suddenly Beach got hot," Shawn continued. "He intercepted one pass that got called back, and not too much later, intercepted another. He was all over the field. It was he and this other guy Fichtner, Ross Fichtner, just wreaking havoc on the Eagles.

"And then, get this, the pièce de résistance," Shawn said, in a way to assure he was reaching the climax of his story because he could sense Bill was just itching to get a word in edgewise.

"When my uncle got mad at me, he called Beach or Brown, I can't remember which, you know...that word. The word that begins with n... the word.

"Yeah, I know the word," Bill answered, just as Amos Otis was coming to the plate to start the ninth inning. "I've had to grapple with that fucking word a lot lately."

"Anyway," Shawn continued, after they both paused just for a second to watch the Cardiac Kids in action, "my mom reached out and smacked him hard...like a shot."

"No! At the game, in front of all those men."

"Yep."

"Oooh," Bill said, imagining the situation and bowling over and rocking back in his chair. "Wow."

When Bill looked back up at Shawn, he realized he'd been enlightened.

"Shawn Berg," he began, before reaching into his pocket for his wallet and looking Shawn straight into his eyes. "I just had an epiphany, my new friend. Not only have you been an unconscious inspiration for me since that day we met, but throughout it all, we've been connected somehow.

"That's the only way I can explain these things," he continued, as he handed Shawn what looked like a business card. "Look at this."

"That's Ali," Shawn said, looking at what was a laminated picture reduced to fit into a wallet."

"That's all you see? Look harder," Bill said, just as McGraw struck out Otis for the first out of the ninth inning.

"Oh, that a young Kareem on the right," Shawn recognized.

"But back then, he was Lew Alcindor. Keep...."

"Oh, that's Jimmy Brown, right there, next to Ali. Nice, what is this."

Bill cradled the picture in his right hand before putting both over his heart and closing his eyes for a second. Then he began pointing.

"Next to Ali on the left there, that's Bill Russell, and right there," he said, pointing to the picture of twelve black men gathered in front of microphones.

"Right there, between Ali and Russell, in the background, you'll never guess who that is," he said circling the subject with his finger.

They both looked up at the screen, before Shawn focused his attention on the eight men standing behind the four stars.

"Willie, all I recognize in this picture is Russell, Ali, Jimmy Brown, and Kareem," he said, looking left to right. I have no idea who those guys in the back are."

"That's Walter Beach," Bill triumphantly pointed to the man again.

"No, really? I don't think I ever really knew what he looked like?"

"I would have never known who Walter Beach was had it not been for this picture. I wasn't that big of a fan of the Browns. I mean, I knew Jim Brown, Leroy Kelly, and Paul Warfield," he said, mentioning the three big-name black athletes from that 1964 championship season.

"What is the picture?" Shawn asked, just as McGraw walked the next batter, Willie Aikens.

"I've only come to realize, Shawn, that I have been unconsciously preparing for this day since I lost sight of you in 1964. First I wanted to be a better musician than you, and at some point when I knew I wasn't good enough to be a pro, I think inside me, when I knew I had to give up making a living making music, I wanted to still be in it. So just in case I saw you again, the young white violin-playing Bizarro World version of me on the other side of town of my non-piano-playing black ass, I wanted to at least make sure I had more money than you."

"Well, you sure succeeded there," Shawn laughed, looking around at the opulence of a private bar inside a major league ballpark. "All that's deep, and what does it have to do with the Walter Beach in this picture."

"After that meeting with Ali, Brown, Sam Cooke, and Malcolm X in '64, I got interested in the idea of marrying the entertainment and sports industry as a way to build black wealth.

"My heroes after that weren't just black athletes and musicians but black music and sports business people who used their wealth to uplift black families and communities. That's why people like Harry Pace at Black Swan and Berry Gordy Jr. at Motown became heroes of mine.

"This picture was another example of black men, all athletes of means furthering exactly what I was thinking," Bill continued, getting more inebriated. "It's called the Cleveland Summit. And I can't believe here in front of me is the myth that was Shawn Berg and you tell me that Jim Brown and Walter Beach are heroes of yours? Mine too. This right here," he continued, and then stopped to look at the television. Kansas City's catcher John Wathan singled to put men at first and second to bring the tying run to the plate in the person of batter Jose Cardenal.

"The Cardiac Kids are at it again," Shawn said, looking up at the picture of the crowd on its feet.

"This picture," Bill pointed, getting the focus back to their past. "This was another attempt at Jim Brown furthering that black economy idea. Stuff like this is why Jim Brown became a hero of mine."

"It helped that he was a bad motherfucker, I'm sure," Shawn interrupted.

"Absolutely," Bill laughed, as they both looked up at the screen to watch the Cardiac Kids wade deeper into trouble. "But I also began developing other kinds of heroes like another bad motherfucker named Abram Lincoln Harris who wrote a book called *The Negro as Capitalist,* and the first black law professor at Harvard, Derrick Bell, who today has positive theories on black economics that I think is the only way for black people to beat racism with dignity.

"And I wanted to have more money than you," he laughed, gripping Shawn on the shoulder. "You started me down this road."

"Don't blame me for that shit," Shawn laughed, again pointing out where they were.

"Man, had George Knox not tried to knock your eye out when we were kids, I could've been a junkie out there on Front Street."

"The pain I had to go through to make you a success."

"But here's the kicker, Shawn Berg," Bill continued, now definitely qualifying as drunk. "Our mothers. You won't believe what else we have in common."

"Yes, we have mothers," Shawn slurred, with the assurance that he too had crossed over into being well-oiled.

Just then Cardenal singled to load the bases with only one out. The whole stadium was nervous. "And this is going to blow your Philadelphia Philly fucking mind," Bill went on, as if he didn't hear Shawn's smart-ass retort or the roaring crowd. "Our mothers both hit white men for saying the word 'nigger.' And the man my mother slapped was a cop!"

"Wha'cha talkin' 'bout, Willis," Shawn slurred through laughter.

"Oh, you watch that show?" Bill asked, about the rising-in-popularity television show *Diff'rent Strokes,* whose third-season premiere was being promoted on NBC during the World Series. The young diminutive star, Gary Coleman, was famous for the line Shawn massacred.

"No, actually, I just heard my wife say it the other day. I said it because she said I need to be hipper. But what are you talking about with your mother."

Time bogged down in the game with a pinch runner, a disputed play, and other distractions. As their eyes darted back and forth between each other and the television monitor, Bill told the incredible story of how Marjorie Jane Malden got so mad that she, without thinking, slapped a known racist Philadelphia police officer. The story had Shawn totally intrigued as he thought of little Willie Malden watching his father and brother fight.

His mind raced thinking of what it must've been like to have a brother growing up. He thought of George Knox and it began to feel surreal that he was actually listening to the guy who he'd always said saved his life. It was his turn to have a revelation as it dawned on him how much that day, and by extension, Little Willie Malden may have influenced his ideas on race.

He listened and reacted in awe as Bill told the story. Inside he chuckled at himself for the peculiarity of the fact that since college the only true black friends he'd had were opera singers, males, females, straight and gay. When he turned pro, he'd been good acquaintances with many black musicians, especially after he started playing with MFSB. *It's a quirk,* he thought, *that those days were now over with an exciting brand-new buddy, like new love.*

Shawn's lightning bolt moment came when he thought about what he heard one of O.J.'s Buddhist friends say about how everyone's connected. It hit him that Bill was right—those moments from childhood seemed to have somehow inextricably linked them. *Wow!* is what he thought, as he combined his thoughts with Bill explaining how he never saw the cop again. However, subconsciously, after thinking of MFSB, something else came out of his mouth.

"Betcha by golly wow," he declared.

Bill cracked up just as Pete Rose made a spectacular play. In foul territory the Phillies' catcher, Bob Boone, chased a pop-up off the bat of Frank White. He caught it, dropped it, but first baseman Rose backed him up and was there, catching the ball near the ground close to the visitors' right-field-line dugout.

"Is that you trying to be hip again like that gorgeous wife of yours?" he slurred. "What do you know about *Betcha by Golly Wow?* It's a

Acknowledgments

Thank you to my tremendous team:
Dr. Valerie Hepburn-Ruffin, Terri Hinte, Steve Watkins, B'Rael Ali,
Pat Lofthouse, Michelle Delacourt, Nick Carter, and Vinessa Currie.
This could not have happened without each one of you.

Thank you for a small, medium, or large dose of inspiration:
Adarsh Alphons, Walter Beach, Gail Boyd, Dee Dee Bridgewater,
Terri Lyne Carrington, Norman Connors, George Freeman, Bette
Gordon, Maxine Gordon, Andre Guess, Terry Spencer Hesser, Malcolm
Jamal-Warner, Willard Jenkins, Ashley Kahn, Ramsey Lewis, Christian
McBride, Lee Mergner, Henry McGee, Eric Mercury, Diana Muchmore,
Project Art, Demond Robertson, Joanna Ruffin, Neal Sapper, Michael
Seltzer, Ben Sidran, Willa Swift, Michael Teevan at Major League
Baseball; Neil Tesser, Gwen Verdon, Billy Walden, and Bridget Wilson.
To my favorite editors: Gale Kappe, *Chicago Magazine;* Laura Emmerick,
Chicago Sun-Times; Jason Koransky, *Down Beat;* David Smallwood,
N'Digo. René Marie and Antonio Adolfo for a push near the finish
line. And my three sons, Kenyatta, Sidney, and Melcolm, who are
a part of everything I do.

In addition to tons of old articles, these books I read helped to influence these stories.

All His Jazz: The Life and Death of Bob Fosse by Martin Gottfried

Razzle Dazzle: The Life and Work of Bob Fosse by Kevin Boyd Grubb

Thelonious Monk: The Life and Times of an American Original by Robin D. G. Kelley

The Fifties by David Halberstam

October 1964 by David Halberstam

The Children by David Halberstam

The 1964 Phillies: The Story of Baseball's Most Memorable Collapse by John P. Rossi

September Swoon: Richie Allen, the '64 Phillies and Racial Integration by William C. Kashatus

Delightfulee: The Life and Music of Lee Morgan by Jeff McMillan

Lee Morgan: His Life, Music and Culture by Tom Perchard

Faces at the Bottom of the Well: The Permanence of Racism by Derrick Bell

About the Author

The release of this volume of stories coincides with the celebration of Mark Ruffin's 40th year in broadcasting and journalism.

Since 2007, the double Emmy winner and Grammy nominee has been the program director of the Real Jazz channel on SiriusXM Satellite Radio. Before that he spent over 25 years as a fixture in jazz broadcasting and journalism in Chicago including winning two Emmy Awards for his efforts in bringing stories about jazz to television on WTTW-TV/Chicago.

Photo by Nick Carter Photography

Mr. Ruffin worked for over 25 years as Jazz Editor for *Chicago Magazine* and has written hundreds of articles on jazz, broadcasting, and African-American culture. His articles have appeared in a variety of local and national publications, including the *Chicago Sun-Times*, *Down Beat*, *Jazziz*, *N'Digo*, *Atlanta Journal-Constitution*, *Playboy*, *Ebony*, and dozens of other publications.

He has produced radio for Oprah Winfrey, Gayle King, Ramsey Lewis, Marcus Miller, Steppenwolf Theatre, Christian McBride, and many more.

He has produced music for René Marie, Charenee Wade, Giacomo Gates, Lauren Henderson, George Freeman, and others.

He is winner of both the Jazz Journalists Association Career Excellence in Broadcasting Award and the Duke Dubois Humanitarian Award from Jazzweek.com. In 2019 he was honored by Jazzmobile with their NYC Jazz Readers Award.

Mr. Ruffin lives in New York City with his wife Valerie and 5000 CDs. *Bebop Fairy Tales: An Historical Fiction Trilogy on Jazz, Intolerance, and Baseball* is his first book.